"Who are you?" he snapped

Ellen froze in shock, then whirled around to face the intruder. Suddenly aware she was clad only in her jeans and bra, she yanked the towel from her wet hair and clasped it to her chest. "Who are *you*?" she snapped in return, her mind envisioning tomorrow's newspaper headline: Woman Assaulted in Kitchen . . . "What are you doing here?" she managed despite her fear.

"This is my home!" he thundered.

"Your home?" Ellen choked out. "But *I* live here . . . with Derek and—"

"Not anymore you don't," he cut in. "I'm Derek's brother, and I'm wondering just how long this cozy setup has been going on."

His implication was clear. Horrified, Ellen stammered, "Derek and I are nothing more than friends!"

"I'll just bet," he said, eyeing her scant attire. "I'll just bet."

Debbie Macomber is an American writer born in the state of Washington, where she still lives. She and her electrician husband have four children from the age of ten years to fifteen. Debbie began writing as a child, her first bestseller being her diary, which her brothers copied—and sold! She has written many magazine articles, and her first novel, written because she fell in love with Harlequin Romances and wanted to write her own, was published in 1982. Since then she has had more than ten published novels in romance lines.

Books by Debbie Macomber

HARLEQUIN ROMANCE
2768—THE MATCHMAKERS

Love
by Degree
Debbie Macomber

Harlequin Books

TORONTO • NEW YORK • LONDON
AMSTERDAM • PARIS • SYDNEY • HAMBURG
STOCKHOLM • ATHENS • TOKYO • MILAN

ISBN 0-373-02835-0

Harlequin Romance first edition May 1987
Second printing May 1987

CHAPTER ONE

THE MELODIOUS SOUNDS of a love ballad drifted softly through the huge three-story house in Seattle's Capitol Hill. Ellen Cunningham hummed the catchy Neil Diamond tune as she rubbed her wet curls with a thick towel. These late-afternoon hours before her housemates returned were the only time she had the place to herself, so she'd taken advantage of the peaceful interlude to leisurely wash her hair. Privacy was at a premium with three men in the house, and she couldn't always count on the upstairs bathroom being available later in the evening.

Twisting the fire-engine-red towel around her head, turban style, Ellen walked barefoot across the hallway toward her bedroom to retrieve her blouse. Halfway there, she heard the faint ding of the oven timer, signaling that her apple pie was ready to come out.

Automatically she altered her course and bounded down the wide stairway, humming as she went. Her classes that day had gone exceptionally well. She couldn't remember ever being happier, even though she still missed Yakima, the small apple-growing community in central Washington, where she'd been raised. But she was adjusting well to life in the big city. She'd waited impatiently for the right time—and enough money—to complete her education, and she'd been gratified by the way everything had suddenly fallen into place during the past summer. Her younger sister had married, and her "baby" brother had entered the military. For a while, Ellen had feared that her mother might suffer from the "empty nest syndrome," so she had decided to delay her education another year. But her worries had been groundless, as it turned out. James Simonson, a widower friend of her mother's, had started dropping by the house often enough for Ellen to recognize a romance brewing between the two. The time was finally ripe for Ellen to make the break, and she did it without guilt or self-reproach.

Clutching a pot holder in one hand, she opened the oven door and lifted out the steaming pie. The fragrance of spicy apples filled the huge kitchen, mingling with the savory aroma of the stew that simmered gently on top of the stove. Carefully, Ellen set the pie on a wire rack that rested on the counter. Her housemates appreciated her culinary efforts and she enjoyed doing little things to please them. As the oldest, Ellen fit easily into this household of young men; in fact, she felt that the arrangement was ideal. In exchange for cooking, a little mothering on the side and a share of the cleaning, Ellen paid only a nominal rent.

The unexpected sound of the back door opening caused her to swivel around sharply.

"What the hell?" The open doorway was dominated by a man with the most piercing green eyes Ellen had ever seen. They reminded her of emeralds caught in the sunlight, flashing now, and intense. She noticed immediately that the rest of his features were strongly defined and perfectly balanced. His cheekbones were high and wide, yet amazingly his face remained lean and appealing. His mouth was twisted in an unspoken question and his forehead was pleated in a thick frown, narrowing the intense eyes.

In one clenched hand he held a large leather suitcase, which he slowly lowered to the kitchen floor. "Who are you?" He spoke sharply, but it wasn't anger or disdain that edged his voice; it was genuine bewilderment.

Ellen was too shocked to move. When she'd whirled around so suddenly, the towel had slipped from her head and covered one eye, blocking her vision. But even a one-eyed view of this stranger was enough to intimidate her. She had to admit that his impeccable three-piece business suit didn't look very threatening—but then she glanced up at his glowering face again.

With as much poise as possible, she raised a hand to straighten the turban and realized that she was standing in the kitchen wearing washed-out jeans and a bright white bra. Grabbing the towel from her head, she clasped it to her chest for protection. "Who are you?" she snapped back. To her chagrin, she realized she must have made a laughable sight, holding a red bath towel in front of her like a matador before a charging bull. This man reminded her of a bull. He was tall, muscular and solidly built. And she somehow knew that when he moved, it would be with effortless power and sudden speed. Not exactly the type of man she'd want to meet in a dark alley. Or a deserted house, for that matter. Already Ellen could see the headlines: Small-Town Girl Assaulted in Capitol Hill Kitchen.

"What are you doing here?" she demanded in her sternest voice.

"This is my home!" The words vibrated around the walls like claps of thunder.

"Your home?" Ellen choked out. "But...I live here."

"Not anymore you don't."

"Who are you?" she demanded a second time.

"Reed Morgan."

Ellen relaxed her defenses. "Derek's brother?"

"Half brother."

No wonder they didn't look anything alike. Derek was a lanky, easy-going nineteen-year-old, with dark hair and equally dark eyes. Ellen would certainly never have expected Derek to have a brother—even a half brother—like this glowering titan.

"I—I didn't know you were coming," she hedged, feeling utterly foolish.

"Apparently." He cocked one brow ever so slightly as he viewed the velvet perfection of her bare shoulders. He shoved the heavy suitcase out of the doorway, then sighed deeply and ran his hands through his hair. Ellen couldn't help making the irrelevant observation that it was a dark auburn, thick and lustrous with health.

He looked tired and irritable. He obviously wasn't in the best frame of mind for any explanations of why she was running around his kitchen half naked. "Would you like a cup of coffee?" she offered congenially, hoping to ease the shock of her presence.

"What I'd like is for you to put some clothes on."

"Yes, of course." Forcing a smile, Ellen turned abruptly and left the kitchen, feeling humiliated that she could stand there discussing coffee with a stranger when she was practically naked. Taking the stairs two at a time, she entered her room and removed the blouse from the end of the bed. Her fingers were trembling as she tried to do up the buttons.

Her thoughts spun in confusion. If this house was indeed Reed Morgan's, then he had every right to ask her to leave. She sincerely hoped he'd made some mistake. Or that she'd misunderstood. It would be difficult to find another place to share this far into the school term. And her meager savings would be quickly wiped out if she had to live someplace on her own. Ellen's brow wrinkled with worry as she dragged a brush through her short, bouncy curls, still slightly damp from washing. Being forced to move wouldn't be a tragedy, but close enough to one that she was understandably apprehensive. The role of housemother came naturally to Ellen. The boys couldn't so much as boil water without her. She'd only recently broken them in to running the vacuum cleaner and the washing machine without her assistance.

When she returned to the kitchen, she found Reed leaning against the counter. His hands hugged a ceramic mug of steaming coffee.

"How long has this cozy setup with you and Derek been going on?"

"About two months now," she answered, pouring herself a cup of coffee. Although she rarely drank it she felt she needed something to occupy her hands. "But it's not what you're implying. Derek and I are nothing more than friends."

"I'll just bet."

Ellen could deal with almost anything except sarcasm. Gritting her teeth until her jaw ached, she replied in an even, controlled voice. "I'm not going to stand here and argue with you. Derek advertised for a housemate and I answered the ad. I came to live here with him and the others and—"

"The others?" Reed blew a mouthful of coffee back into the mug. "You mean there's more of you around?"

Expelling her breath slowly in an effort to maintain her calm, Ellen boldly met his scowl. "There's Derek, Pat and—"

"Is Pat male or female?" The sheer force of his personality filled the kitchen. But Ellen refused to be intimidated.

"Pat is a male friend who attends classes at the university with Derek and me."

"So you're all students?"

"Yes."

He eyed her curiously. "Aren't you a bit old for the college scene?"

"I'm twenty-four." She wasn't about to explain her circumstances to this man.

The sound of the front door opening and closing directed their attention to the opposite end of the house. Carrying an armload of books, Derek Morgan sauntered into the kitchen and stopped cold when he caught sight of his older brother.

"Hi, Reed." Uncertain eyes flew to Ellen as if seeking reassurance. A worried look pinched the boyishly handsome face. Slowly, he placed his books on top of the counter.

"Derek."

"I see you've met Ellen." Derek's welcoming smile was decidedly forced and looked as brittle as old parchment.

"We more or less stumbled into each other." Derek's stiff shoulders relaxed as Reed straightened and set the mug aside.

"I didn't expect you back so soon."

Momentarily, Reed's gaze slid to Ellen. "That much is obvious. Do you want to tell me what's going on here, little brother?"

"It's not as bad is it appears."

"Right now it doesn't look particularly good."

"I can explain everything."

"I'm hoping that's possible."

Nervously swinging her arms at her sides, Ellen stepped forward. "If you two will excuse me, I'll be up in my room." The last thing she wanted was to find herself positioned between the two brothers while they settled their differences.

"No, don't go," Derek said quickly. His dark eyes urgently pleaded with her to stay.

Almost involuntarily Ellen glanced at Reed for guidance.

"By all means, stay." But his look wasn't encouraging.

A growing sense of resentment made her arch her back and thrust out her chin defiantly. Who was this...this unnerving male to burst into their tranquil lives and raise havoc? The four lived congenially together, all of them doing their parts in the smooth running of the household.

"Are you charging rent?" Reed demanded.

Briefly Derek's eyes met Ellen's. "It makes sense, doesn't it? This big old house has as many bedrooms as a dorm. I didn't think it would hurt." He swallowed nervously. "I mean with you being in the Middle East and all. The house was...so empty."

"How much are you paying?" Reed directed the question to Ellen. That sarcastic look was back and Ellen resisted the urge to give him the good tongue-lashing he deserved.

"How much?" Reed repeated when she hesitated.

Ellen knew just from the way Derek's eyes widened that they were entering into dangerous territory.

"It's different with Ellen," Derek hurried on to explain. "She does all the shopping and the cooking, so the rest of us—"

"Are you sure that's all she provides?" Reed interrupted harshly.

Ellen's gaze didn't waver. "I pay ten dollars a week, but believe me, I earn my keep." The second the words slipped out, Ellen wanted to take them back.

"I'm sure you do."

Ellen was too furious and outraged to speak. How dare he just barge into this house and immediately assume the worst? All right, she'd been walking around half naked, but she hadn't exactly been expecting company.

Angrily Derek stepped forward. "It's not like that, Reed."

"I discovered her prancing around in the kitchen in her bra. What else am I supposed to think?"

Derek groaned and cast an accusing look at Ellen. "I just ran down to get the pie out of the oven," she asserted in her own defense.

"Let me assure you," Derek said, his voice quavering with righteousness. "You've got this all wrong." He glared indignantly at his older brother. "Ellen isn't that kind of woman. I resent the implication. As far as I'm concerned, you owe us both an apology."

From the stunned look on Reed's face, Ellen surmised that this could well be the first time Derek had stood up to his domineering older brother. Her impulse was to clap her hands and shout: "That a boy!" With an immense effort she restrained herself.

Reed wiped a hand over his face and pinched the bridge of his nose. "Perhaps I do at that."

The front door opened and closed again. "Anyone here?" Monte's eager voice rang from the living room. The sound of his books hitting the stairs echoed through the narrow hallway that led into the kitchen. "Something smells good." Skidding to an abrupt halt just inside the room, the tall freshman looked around at the somber faces. "What's going on? You three look like you're about to attend a funeral."

"Are you Pat?" Reed asked.

"No, Monte."

Reed closed his eyes and wearily rubbed the back of his neck. "Just how many bedrooms have you rented out?"

Derek lowered his gaze to his hands. "Three."

"My room?" Reed questioned.

"Yes, well, Ellen needed a place and it seemed only logical to give her that one. You were supposed to be gone a year or so. What happened?"

"I came home early."

Abruptly stepping forward, her fingers nervously laced together, Ellen broke into the tense interchange between the two men. "I'll move up a floor. I don't mind, really." The third floor of the older house had once been reserved for the servants. The rooms were small and airless, but sleeping there was preferable to suffering the wrath of Derek's brother. Or worse, being forced to find someplace else to live.

Reed responded with a dismissive gesture of his hand. "Don't worry about it. Until things are straightened out, I'll sleep up there. Once I've taken a long, hot shower and gotten some rest I might be able to make some sense out of this mess."

"No, please." Ellen persisted. "If I'm in your room, then it's only right that I move."

"No," Reed grumbled on his way out the door, waving aside her offer. "It's only my house. I'll sleep in the servants' quarters."

Before Ellen could argue further, Reed was out of the kitchen and halfway up the stairs.

"Is there a problem?" Monte asked, opening the refrigerator. He didn't appear particularly concerned, but then he rarely worried about anything unless it directly affected his stomach. Ellen didn't know how any one person could eat so much. His build was strong and lithe, and he never seemed to gain weight, but if it were up to him he'd feed himself exclusively on pizza and French fries.

"Do you want to explain what's going on?" Ellen pressed Derek, feeling guilty but not quite knowing why. "I assumed your family owned the house."

"Well . . . sort of," he hedged, sinking slowly into one of the kitchen chairs.

"It's the *sort of* that worries me." She pulled out the chair across from Derek and looked at him sternly.

"Reed is family."

"But he didn't know that you were renting out the bedrooms?"

"He told me this job would last nine months to a year. I couldn't see any harm in doing it. Everywhere I looked there were ads for students wanting rooms to rent. It didn't seem right to live alone in this house with all these bedrooms."

"Maybe I should start looking for someplace else to live," Ellen suggested reluctantly. The more she thought about it, the harder it was to see any other solution now that Reed had returned.

"Not before dinner," Monte protested, delivering a loaf of bread and assorted sandwich makings to the table.

"There's no need for anyone to leave," Derek returned with defiant bravado. Three thick lines marred his brow. "Reed will probably only be around a couple of weeks before he goes away on another assignment."

"Assignment?" Ellen questioned, her curiosity piqued.

"Yeah. He travels all over the place—we hardly ever see him. And from what I hear, I don't think Danielle likes him being gone so much, either."

"Danielle?"

"They've been practically engaged for ages and . . . I don't know the whole story, but apparently Reed's been putting off tying the knot because he does so much traveling."

"Danielle must care a great deal for him to be willing to wait." Ellen watched as Monte spread several layers of smoked ham over the inch-thick slice of Swiss cheese. She knew better than to warn her housemate that he would ruin his dinner. After the triple-decker sandwich, Monte could sit down to a five-course meal—and then ask about dessert.

"I guess," Derek answered nonchalantly. "Reed's perfect for her. You'd have to meet Danielle to understand." Reaching into the teddy-bear-shaped cookie jar and helping himself to a handful, Derek continued. "Reed didn't mean to snap at everyone. Usually, he's a super brother. And Danielle's all right," he added without much enthusiasm.

"It takes a special kind of woman to stick by a man that long without a commitment."

Derek shrugged his shoulders. "I suppose. Danielle's got her own reasons, if you know what I mean."

Ellen wasn't sure, but she didn't press. "What does Reed do?"

"He's an aeronautical engineer for Boeing. He travels around the world working on different projects. This last one was somewhere near Saudi Arabia."

"What about the house?"

"Well, that's his, an inheritance from his mother's family, but he's gone so much of the time that he asked me if I would live here and look after the place."

"What about us?" Monte wanted to know, revealing his concern for the first time. "Will big brother want us to move out?"

"I don't think so. Tomorrow morning I'll ask him. I can't see me all alone in this huge old place. It's not like I'm trying to make a fortune by collecting a lot of rent."

"If Reed wants us to leave, then I'm sure something can be arranged." Already Ellen's mind was working. She didn't want her fate to be determined by a whim of Derek's brother.

"Let's not do anything drastic. I don't think he'll mind once he has a chance to think it through," Derek murmured with a thoughtful frown. "At least, I hope not."

Later that night as Ellen slipped between the crisply laundered sheets, she wondered about the strange man whose bed she occupied. Tucking the thick quilt around her shoulders, she battled down a wave of anxiety. Everything had worked out so perfectly that she should have expected something to go wrong. If anyone voiced objections to Reed's renting out bedrooms, it would probably be his almost-fiancée. Ellen sighed apprehensively. She had to admit that if the positions were reversed, she wouldn't want the man she loved sharing his house with another woman. Tomorrow she'd check around to see if she could find a new place to live.

ELLEN WAS SCRAMBLING EGGS the following morning when Reed appeared, coming down the narrow stairs that led from the third floor to the kitchen. He'd shaved, which emphasized the lean chiseled look of his jaw. His handsome face was weathered and everything about him spoke of health and vitality. Ellen paused, her fork suspended in midstroke with raw egg dripping from the tines. She wouldn't call Reed Morgan handsome so much as striking. He had an unmistakable masculine appeal that wouldn't go unnoticed by the female population. Apparently the duties of an aeronautical engineer were more physically demanding than she'd suspected. Strength showed in the wide muscular shoulders and lean, hard build. He looked even more formidable this morning.

"Good morning," she greeted him cheerfully, as she continued to beat the eggs. "I hope you slept well."

Reed poured coffee into the same mug he'd used the day before. A creature of habit, Ellen mused. "Morning," he responded somewhat gruffly.

"Can I fix you some eggs?"

"Derek and I have already talked. You can all stay."

"Is that a yes or a no to the eggs?"

"I'm trying to tell you that you don't need to worry about impressing me with your culinary efforts."

With a grunt of impatience, Ellen set the bowl aside and leaned forward, slapping her open palms down on the countertop. "I'm scrambling eggs here. Whether you want some or not is entirely up to you. Believe me, if I was concerned about getting on your good side, I wouldn't do it with eggs."

For the first time, Ellen saw a hint of amusement touch those brilliant green eyes. "No, I don't suppose you would."

"Now that we've got that settled, would you like breakfast or not?"

"All right."

His eyes boldly searched hers and for an instant Ellen found herself regretting that there was a Danielle. With an effort, she turned away and forced her concentration back to the mechanics of cooking breakfast. This man's potency, his sheer intensity, was making her cautious.

"Do you do all the cooking?" Just the way he asked made it sound as though he were already criticizing their household arrangements. Ellen bit back a sarcastic reply and busied herself melting butter and putting bread in the toaster. She'd bide her time. If Derek was right, his brother would soon be away on another assignment.

"Most of it," Ellen answered, pouring the eggs into the hot skillet.

"Who pays for the groceries?"

Ellen shrugged, hoping to give the appearance of non-chalance. "We all chip in." She did the shopping and most of the cooking. In return, the boys did the majority of the housework.

The bread popped up from the toaster and Ellen reached for the butter knife, doing her best to ignore the overpowering presence of Reed Morgan.

"What about the shopping?"

"I enjoy it," she stated simply, putting two more slices of bread into the toaster.

"I thought women all over America were fighting to get out of the kitchen."

"When a replacement is found, I'll be pleased to move aside." She wasn't comfortable with the direction this conversation seemed to be taking. Reed was looking at her as though she were some kind of museum piece.

"Leave it to Derek to stumble onto another Betty Crocker."

Ellen wasn't amused. She liked to cook, but that didn't make her an antique. As it turned out, the boys needed someone who knew her way around a kitchen, and she needed an inexpensive place to live. Everything had worked out perfectly and she wasn't about to let Reed ruin it now.

She carefully spooned the cooked eggs onto one platter and piled the toast on another, then carried it to the table, which gave her enough time to control her indignation. She was a modern woman who just happened to fit into the role of surrogate mother to a bunch of college-age boys. All right, maybe that made her a little unusual these days, but she enjoyed living with Derek and the others. It helped her feel at home, and for now she needed that.

"Aren't you going to eat?" Reed stopped her on her way out of the kitchen.

"I'll fix myself something later. The only time I can count on the bathroom being free in the mornings is when the boys are having breakfast. That is, unless you were planning to use it?"

Reed's eyes narrowed fractionally. "No."

"What's the matter? You've got that look about you again."

"What look?"

"The one that pinches your lips together as if you aren't pleased about something and are wondering just how much you should say."

The tight expression relaxed into a slow, sensual grin. "Do you always read people this well?"

Ellen shook her head. "Not always. I just want to know what I've done this time."

"Aren't you concerned about living with three men?"

"No. Should I be?" She crossed her arms and leaned against the doorjamb, almost enjoying their conversation. The earlier antagonism had disappeared. She'd agree that her living arrangements were a bit unconventional, but there weren't any strings attached and was mutually advantageous.

"Any one of them could fall in love with you."

With difficulty, Ellen restrained her laughter. "That's unlikely. They see me as their mother."

The corners of his mouth formed deep grooves as he tried—and failed—to suppress a taunting grin. Cocking one thick brow, he did a thorough inspection of her womanly curves, pausing at the full swell of her breasts.

Hot color flooded her pale cheeks. "All right—a sister. I'm too old for the boys."

Monte sauntered into the kitchen, followed closely by Pat. Typically, Pat carried a basketball under his arm. Ellen sometimes wondered if he slept with it as well. "I thought I smelled breakfast."

"I was just about to call you," she told the two and slipped quietly from the room, wanting to avoid a head-on collision with Reed. And that was where this conversation was going.

Fifteen minutes later, Ellen returned to the kitchen. She was dressed in cords and an Irish cable-knit sweater; the soft dark curls framed her small oval face. Ellen had no illusions about her looks. Men on the street weren't going to stop and stare, but she knew she was reasonably attractive. With short, dark hair and deep brown eyes, she considered herself boringly average. Far too ordinary to hold the affection of a man like Reed Morgan. One look at Ellen, and Danielle would feel completely reassured. Angry at the self-pitying thought, she grabbed a pen and tore out a sheet of notebook paper.

Intent on making up the shopping list, Ellen was halfway into the kitchen before she noticed Reed standing at the sink, wiping the frying pan dry. The table had been cleared and the dishes were stacked on the counter, ready for the dishwasher.

"Oh," she said, sounding a little startled. "I would have done that."

"While I'm here, I'll do my share." He said it without looking at her, his eyes avoiding hers.

"But this is your home. I certainly don't mind—"

"I wouldn't be comfortable otherwise. Haven't you got a class this morning?" He sounded anxious to be rid of her.

"Not until eleven."

"What's your major?" He'd turned around, leaning against the sink and crossing his arms over his broad chest. He was the picture of nonchalance, but Ellen wasn't fooled. She knew very well that he wasn't exactly pleased about her living in his home, and she felt he'd given his permission reluctantly. She suspected he was even looking for ways to dislike her. Ellen understood that. Reed was bound to face some awkward questions once Danielle discovered there was a woman living in his house. Especially a woman who slept in his bed and took charge of his kitchen. But that would change this afternoon—at least the sleeping in his bed part.

"I'm majoring in education."

"That's the mother in you coming out again."

Ellen hadn't thought of it that way. Living with the boys hadn't made her matronly. Reed simply felt more comfortable seeing her in that light, she decided. She'd let him, if it meant he'd be willing to accept her arrangement with Derek and the others. Besides he probably wouldn't be around long and then the happy household could go back to its comfortable existence.

"I suppose you're right," she murmured as she began opening and closing cupboard doors, checking the contents on each shelf, and scribbling down several items she'd be needing the following week.

"What are you doing now?"

Mentally, Ellen counted to ten before answering. She resented his overbearing tone, and despite her earlier resolve to humor him, she snapped, "I'm making a grocery list. Do you have a problem with that?"

"No," he answered somewhat gruffly.

"I'll be out of here in just a minute," she said, trying hard to maintain her patience.

"You aren't in my way."

"And while we're on the subject of being in someone's way, I want you to know I plan to move my things out of your room this afternoon."

"Don't. I doubt that I'll be here long enough to make it worth your while."

CHAPTER TWO

So Reed was leaving. Ellen felt guilty and relieved all at the same time. Derek had told her Reed would probably be sent on another job soon, but she hadn't expected it to be quite this soon.

"There's another project Boeing is sending me on. California this time—the Monterey area."

Resuming her task, Ellen added several more items to the grocery list. "I've heard that's a lovely part of the state."

"It is beautiful." But his voice held no enthusiasm.

Ellen couldn't help feeling a twinge of disappointment for Reed. One look convinced her he didn't want to leave again. After all, he'd just returned from several months in the Middle East and already he had another assignment awaiting him in California. If he was dreading this latest job, Ellen could well imagine how Danielle must feel.

"Nonetheless, I think it's important to give you back your room. I'll move my things this afternoon." She'd ask the boys to help and it wouldn't take long.

With his arms crossed over his chest, Reed lounged against the doorjamb, watching her.

"And if you feel that my being here is a problem," she went on, thinking of Danielle, "I'll look for another place. The only thing I ask is that you give me a couple of weeks to find something."

He hesitated as though he were considering the offer, then shook his head, grinning slightly. "I don't think that'll be necessary."

"I don't mind telling you that I'm relieved to hear it, but I'm prepared to move if necessary."

His left brow rose a fraction of an inch as the grin spread across his face. "Having you around does have certain advantages."

Ellen hesitated. "Such as?"

"You're an excellent cook, the house hasn't been this clean in months and Derek's mother thinks you're a wonder with these boys."

Ellen had briefly met Mary Morgan, Derek's mother, a few weeks before. "Thank you."

He sauntered over to the coffeepot and lazily poured himself a cup. "And for that matter, Derek's right. This house is too big to sit empty. I'm often out of town, but there isn't any reason why others shouldn't put it to good use. Especially with someone as...domestically inclined as you around to keep things running smoothly."

So he viewed her as little more than a live-in housekeeper and cook! Ellen felt a flush of anger tint her cheeks. Before she could say something she'd regret, she turned quickly and fled out the back door on her way to the local grocery. Actually, Reed Morgan had interpreted the situation correctly, but it somehow bothered her that he saw her in such an unflattering light.

ELLEN DIDN'T SEE REED again until late that night. Friday evenings were lazy ones for her. She'd dated Charlie Hanson, a fellow student, a couple of times but usually preferred the company of a good book. With her heavy class schedule, most of Ellen's free time was devoted to her studies. Especially algebra. This one class was getting her down. It didn't seem to matter how hard she hit the books, she couldn't understand the theory.

Dressed in her housecoat and a pair of bright purple knee socks, she sat at the kitchen table, propping her legs on the chair across from her. Holding a paperback novel open with one hand, she dipped chocolate-chip cookies into a tall glass of milk with the other. At the unexpected sound of the back door opening, she looked curiously up from her book.

Reed seemed surprised to see her. He frowned as his eyes darted past her to the clock above the stove. "You're up late."

"On weekends my mommy doesn't make me go to bed until midnight," she said sarcastically, doing her best to ignore him. Reed managed to look fantastic without so much as trying. He didn't need her gawking at him to tell him that. If his expensive sports jacket was anything to judge by, he'd spent the evening with Danielle.

"You've got that look about you," he grumbled.

"What look?"

"The same one you claim I have—wanting to say something and unsure if you should or not."

"Oh." She couldn't very well deny it.

"And you wanted to tell me something?"

"Only that you look good." She paused, wondering how much she should say. "You even smell expensive."

His gaze slid over her in a slow inspection. "From the way you're dressed, you look to me as though you'd smell of cotton candy."

"Thank you, but actually it's chocolate chip." She pushed the package of cookies in his direction. "Here. Save me from myself."

"No, thanks," Reed murmured and headed toward the living room.

"Don't go in there," Ellen cried, swinging her legs off the chair and coming abruptly to her feet.

Reed's hand was on the kitchen door, ready to swing it open. "Don't go into the living room?"

"Derek's got a girl in there."

Reed continued to stare at her blankly. "So?"

"So. He's with Michelle Tanner. *The* Michelle Tanner. The very girl Derek's been crazy about for the last six weeks. She finally agreed to a date with him. They rented a movie."

"That doesn't explain why I can't go in there."

"Yes, it does," Ellen whispered. "The last time I peeked, Derek was getting ready to make his move. You'll ruin everything if you barge in there now."

"His move?" Reed didn't seem to like the sound of this. "What do you mean, 'his move'? The kid's barely nineteen."

A soft smile turned up the edges of Ellen's mouth. "Honestly, Reed, you must have been young once. Don't you remember what it's like to have a crush on a girl? All Derek's doing is plotting that first all-important kiss."

Reed dropped his hand as he stared at Ellen. His eyes narrowed and seemed to focus on her mouth. Then the glittering green eyes skimmed hers, and Ellen's breath caught someplace between her throat and her lungs as she struggled to pull her gaze away from his. Reed had no business giving her that kind of look. Not when he'd so recently left Danielle's arms. And not when Ellen reacted so profoundly to a mere glance.

"I haven't forgotten," he murmured. "And as for that remark about being young once, I'm not exactly over the hill."

This was ridiculous! With a sigh of annoyance, Ellen sat down again, swinging her feet onto the opposite chair.

She picked up her book and forced her eyes—if not her attention—back to the page in front of her. "I'm glad to hear that." If she could get a grip on herself for the next few days everything would be fine. Reed would leave and her life with the boys would settle back into its routine once again.

The sound of the refrigerator opening and closing drew her gaze. She watched as Reed poured himself a glass of milk and then reached for a handful of chocolate-chip cookies. When he pulled out the chair across from her, Ellen reluctantly lowered her legs.

"What are you reading?"

Feeling irritable and angry for allowing him to affect her, she deliberately waited until she'd finished the page before answering. "A book," she muttered.

"My, my, you're a regular Mary Sunshine. What's the matter—did your boyfriend stand you up tonight?"

With exaggerated patience she slowly lowered the paperback to the table and marked her place. "Listen. I'm twenty-four years old and whole light-years beyond the age of boyfriends."

Reed shrugged. "All right. Your lover."

The air caught in her lungs, strangling off a reply. She hadn't meant to imply that at all. And Reed knew it. He'd wanted to fluster her and he'd succeeded.

"Women these days have this habit of letting their jaws hang open," he said pointedly, staring at her. "I suppose they think it looks sexy, but actually, they resemble beached trout." With that, he deposited his empty glass in the sink and marched briskly up the back stairs.

Ellen closed her eyes and groaned in embarrassment. He must think her a world-class idiot, and with good reason. She'd done a remarkable job of imitating one.

She groaned again, infuriated by the fact that she found Reed Morgan so damned attractive.

Ellen didn't climb the stairs to her new bedroom on the third floor for another hour. And then it was only after Derek had paid her a quick visit in the kitchen and given her the thumbs-up sign. At least his night had gone well.

Long after she'd turned off her reading lights, Ellen lay staring into the silent, shadow-filled room. She wasn't in the least sleepy, and the mystery novel no longer held her interest. Her thoughts were troubled by that brief incident in the kitchen with Reed. Burying her head in the thick feather pillow, Ellen yawned and closed her eyes. But sleep still wouldn't come. A half-hour later, she threw back the covers and grabbed the housecoat from the end of the bed. Perhaps a glass of milk would help.

Not bothering to turn on any lights, she took a clean glass from the dishwasher and pulled the carton of milk from the refrigerator. With her drink in her hand, she stood at the kitchen window, looking out at the huge oak tree in the backyard. Its bare limbs stretched upward like skeletal hands, silhouetted against the full moon.

"I've heard that a woman's work is never done, but this is ridiculous."

She nearly spilled her milk at the sudden sound of Reed's low voice behind her. She whirled around and glared at him hotly. "I see there's a full moon tonight. I wonder if it's safe to be alone with you. And wouldn't you know it, I left my silver bullet upstairs."

"No woman's ever accused me of being a werewolf. Several other things," he murmured tightly, "but never that."

"Maybe that's because you hadn't frightened them half out of their wits."

"I couldn't resist. Sorry," he grumbled, reaching for the milk carton.

"You know, if we'd stop snapping at each other, it might make things a lot easier around here."

"Perhaps," he agreed reluctantly. "I will admit it's a whole lot easier to talk to you when you're dressed."

Ellen slammed down her empty glass and spoke through clenched teeth. "I'm getting a little tired of hearing about that."

But Reed went on, unperturbed. "Unfortunately, ever since that first time when I found you in your bra, you've insisted on overdressing. Do you always wear socks to bed?"

"Usually."

"I pity the man you sleep with."

"Well, you needn't worry..." She hesitated and expelled a lungful of oxygen. "We're arguing again."

"So, you're suggesting we stop trading insults for the sake of the children."

An involuntary smile touched her full mouth. "I hadn't thought to put it that way, but you're right. No one's going to be comfortable if the two of us are constantly snapping at each other. I'm willing to try if you are. Agreed?"

"All right." A smile softened Reed's features, harsh and shadowed in the moonlight.

"And I'm not a threat to you and Danielle, am I? In fact, if you'd rather, she need never even know I'm here," she suggested casually.

"Maybe that would have been best," he conceded, setting aside his empty glass. "But I doubt it. Besides, she already knows. I told her tonight." He grumbled disparagingly something else that she didn't catch.

"And?" Ellen coaxed.

"And," he breathed, "she said she doesn't mind in the least, but she'd like to meet you."

This was one confrontation Ellen wasn't going to enjoy.

THE FOLLOWING MORNING, Ellen brought down her laundry and was running the washing machine and the dryer before Reed or the others were even awake.

She grumbled disparagingly as she tested the iron with the wet tip of her index finger and found that it still wasn't hot, although she'd turned it on at least five minutes earlier. This house was owned by a wealthy engineer, so why were there only two electrical outlets in the kitchen? It meant that she couldn't use the washer, the dryer and the iron at the same time without causing a brownout.

"Damn," she muttered, setting the iron upright on the padded board.

"What's the matter?" Reed asked from the doorway leading into the kitchen. He ambled over to the coffeepot and poured himself a cup.

"This iron."

"Say, Ellen, if you've got some ironing to do, would you mind pressing a few things for me?" Monte asked, walking barefoot into the kitchen. He paused at the refrigerator and took out a slice of cold pizza.

"I was afraid this would happen," she grumbled, still upset by the house's electrical problems.

"Ellen's not your personal maid," Reed interrupted harshly. "If you've got something you want pressed, do it yourself."

A hand on her hip, Ellen turned to Reed, defiantly meeting his glare. "If you don't mind, I can answer for myself."

"Fine," he snorted and took a sip of the hot coffee.

She directed her next words to Monte, who stood looking at her expectantly. "I'm not your personal maid. If you want something pressed, do it yourself."

Monte glanced from Reed to Ellen and back to Reed again. "I'm sorry I asked," he mumbled on his way out of the kitchen. The door was left swinging in his wake.

"You said that well," Reed commented with a soft chuckle.

"Believe me, I was conned into enough schemes by my sister and brother to know how to handle Monte and the others."

Reed's gaze was admiring. "If your brother is anything like mine, I don't doubt it."

"All brothers are alike," she said. Unable to hold back a grin, Ellen tested the iron a second time and noted that it was only slightly warmer. "Have you ever thought about putting another outlet in this kitchen?"

Reed's returning glance revealed surprise. "No. Do you need one?"

"Need one?" she flared. "There are only two for this room. It's ridiculous."

Reed scanned the kitchen. "I hadn't thought about it." Setting his coffee mug aside, he shook his head. "Your mood's not much better today than it was last night." With that remark, he quickly left the room, following in Monte's footsteps.

Ellen unconsciously tightened her grip on the iron as the frustration worked its way through her. Reed was right, of course. She was behaving like a regular shrew and she really didn't understand why. But she was honest enough to admit, at least to herself, that she was attracted to this man whose house she occupied. She realized she'd have to erect a wall of reserve between them to protect them both from embarrassment.

"Morning, Ellen," Derek said as he sauntered into the kitchen and swung his lithe frame into a chair. As he emptied a box of cornflakes into a huge bowl, he casually announced, "Say, I've got some shirts that need pressing."

"If you want anything pressed, do it yourself," she fairly shouted.

Stunned, Derek blinked twice. "Okay."

Setting the iron upright, Ellen released a lengthy sigh. "I didn't mean to scream at you."

"That's all right."

Turning off the iron, she joined Derek at the table and reached for the cornflakes.

"Are you still worried about that math paper you're supposed to do?"

"I'm working my way to an early grave over it."

"I would have thought you'd do well in math."

Ellen snickered. "Hardly."

"Have you come up with a topic?"

"Not yet. I'm going to the library later, where I pray some form of inspiration will strike me."

"Have you asked the others in your class what they're writing about?" Derek asked as he refilled his bowl, this time with rice puffs.

Disgruntled, Ellen nodded her head. "That's what worries me most. The brain who sits beside me is doing hers on the probability of solving Goldbach's conjecture in our lifetime."

Derek's eyes widened. "That's a tough act to follow."

"If that overwhelms you, let me tell you about the guy who sits behind me. He's doing his paper on mathematics during World War II."

"You're in the big league now," Derek muttered with a sympathetic shake of his head.

"I know," Ellen lamented. She was taking this course only because it was compulsory; all she wanted out of it was a passing grade. The quadratic formula certainly wasn't going to have any lasting influence on her life.

"Good luck," Derek offered.

"Thanks, I'm going to need it."

After straightening up the kitchen, Ellen changed into old jeans and a faded sweatshirt. The jeans had been washed so many times the blue was nearly gone. They fit her hips so snugly she could hardly slide her fingers into the pockets, but she hated the idea of throwing them away.

She tied an old red scarf around her hair and headed for the garage. While rooting around there for a ladder a few days earlier, she'd discovered some pruning shears. In the backyard she'd noticed several overgrown bushes that needed trimming and she decided to tackle those first, before cleaning the downspouts.

After an hour, she had a pile of underbrush large enough to be worth a haul to the dump. She'd have one of the boys do that later. For now, the downspouts demanded her attention.

"Derek," she called as she pushed open the back door. Her faced was flushed with exertion and a light film of perspiration wet her upper lip.

"Yeah?" His voice drifted toward her from the living room.

Ellen wandered into the room to discover him on the phone. "I'm ready for you now."

"Now?" His eyes pleaded with her as his palm cupped the telephone mouthpiece. "It's Michelle."

"All right, I'll catch Monte."

"Thanks." He tossed her a smile of appreciation.

But Monte was nowhere to be found, and Pat was at the YMCA shooting baskets with some friends. When she stuck her head into the living room again, she saw Derek still draped over the sofa, deep in conversation. Unwilling to interfere with the course of young love, she decided she could probably manage to climb onto the roof unaided.

Dragging the aluminum ladder from the garage, she speculated that she might not need Derek's help anyway. She'd mentioned her plan earlier in the week, and he hadn't looked particularly enthusiastic. But when it came to chores, none of the boys were eager volunteers.

With the extension ladder braced against the side of the house, she climbed onto the roof of the back porch. Very carefully, she reached for the ladder and pulled it to that level before extending it to the very top of the house.

She maneuvered herself back onto the ladder and climbed slowly and cautiously up.

Once she'd managed to position herself on the slanting roof, she was fine. She even took a moment to enjoy the spectacular view. She could see Lake Washington, with its deep-green water, and the spacious grounds of the university campus.

Using the whisk broom she'd tucked—with some struggle—into her back pocket, Ellen began clearing away the leaves and other debris that clogged the gutters and downspouts.

She was about half finished when she heard raised voices from below. Pausing, she sat down, drawing her knees against her chest, and watched the scene unfolding on the front lawn. Reed and his brother were obviously embroiled in a heated discussion—with Reed doing most of the talking. Derek was raking leaves and didn't look the least bit pleased about devoting his Saturday morning to chores. Ellen guessed that Reed had summarily interrupted the telephone conversation between Derek and Michelle.

With a lackadaisical swish of the rake, Derek flung the multicolored leaves skyward. Ellen restrained a laugh. From the looks of things, Reed was giving him a good scolding.

To her further amusement, Reed then motioned toward his black Porsche, apparently suggesting that his brother wash the car when he'd finished with the leaves. Still chuckling, Ellen reached for the whisk broom, but she missed and accidentally sent it tumbling down the side of the roof. It hit the green shingles over the front porch with a loud thump before flying onto the grass only a few feet from where Derek and Reed were standing.

Two pairs of astonished eyes swiftly turned in her direction. "Hi," she called down and waved. "I don't suppose I could talk one of you into bringing that up to me?" She carefully braced her feet and pulled herself to a standing position as she waited for a reply.

Reed pointed his finger at her and yelled, "What the bloody hell are you doing up there?"

"Playing tiddlywinks," she shouted back. "What do you think I'm doing?"

"I don't know, but I want you down."

"In a minute."

"Now."

"Yes, *sir*." She gave him a mocking salute and would have clicked her heels had she not feared that she might lose her footing.

Derek burst out laughing but was quickly silenced by a scathing glance from his older brother.

"Tell Derek to bring me the broom," Ellen called, moving closer to the edge.

Ellen couldn't decipher Reed's response, but from the way he stormed around the back of the house, she figured it was best to come down before he had a heart attack. She had the ladder lowered to the back-porch roof before she saw him.

"You idiot," he shouted. He was standing in the driveway, his hands positioned challengingly on his hips, glaring at her in fury. "I can't believe anyone would do anything so stupid."

"What do you mean?" The calmness of her words belied the way the blood pulsed through her veins. Alarm thickened his voice and that surprised her. She certainly hadn't expected Reed, of all people, to be concerned about her safety. He held the ladder steady until she'd climbed down and was standing squarely planted on the ground in front of him. Then he started pacing. For a minute Ellen didn't know what to think.

"What's wrong?" she asked. "You look as pale as a sheet."

"What's wrong?" he sputtered. "You were on the *roof* and—"

"I wasn't in any danger." Her brow wrinkled in confusion as she studied his ashen face.

"Like hell," he shouted, clearly upset. "There are people who specialize in that sort of thing. I don't want you up there again. Understand?"

"Yes, but—"

"No buts. You do anything that stupid again and you're out of here. Have you got that?"

"Yes," she said with forced calm. "I understand."

"Good."

Before she could think of anything else to say, Reed was gone.

"You all right?" Derek asked a minute later. Shocked by Reed's unprovoked outburst, Ellen hadn't moved. Rarely had anyone been that angry with her. Heavens, she'd cleaned out downspouts lots of times. Her father had died when Ellen was fourteen, and over the years she'd assumed most of the maintenance duties around the house. She'd quickly learned that, with the help of a good book and a well-stocked hardware store, there wasn't anything she couldn't fix. She'd repaired the plumbing, built bookshelves and done a multitude of household projects. It was an accepted part of her life. Reed had acted as though she'd done something hazardous, as though she'd taken some extraordinary risk, and that seemed totally ridiculous to her. She knew what she was doing. Besides, heights didn't frighten her; they never had.

"Ellen?" Derek prompted.

"I'm fine."

"I've never seen Reed act like that. He didn't mean anything."

"I know," she whispered, brushing the dirt from her knees. Derek drifted off, leaving her to return the ladder to the garage single-handed.

Reed found her an hour later folding laundry in her bedroom. He knocked on the open door.

"Yes?" She looked up expectantly.

"I owe you an apology."

She continued folding towels at the foot of the single bed. "Oh?"

"I didn't mean to come at you like Attila the Hun."

Hugging a University of Washington T-shirt to her stomach, she lowered her gaze to the bedspread and nodded. "Apology accepted and I'll offer one of my own. I didn't mean to come back at you like a spoiled brat."

"Accepted." They smiled at each other and she caught her breath as those incredible green eyes gazed into hers. It was a repeat of the scene in the kitchen the night before. For a long, silent moment they did nothing but stare, and she realized that a welter of conflicting emotions must have registered on her face. A similar turmoil raged on his.

"If it'll make you feel any better, I won't go up on the roof again," she said at last.

"I'd appreciate it." His lips barely moved. The words were more of a sigh than a sentence.

She managed a slight nod in response.

At the sound of footsteps, they guiltily looked away.

"Say, Ellen." Pat stopped in the doorway, the basketball under his left arm. "Have you got time to shoot a few baskets with me?"

"Sure," she whispered, stepping around Reed. At that moment, she'd have agreed to just about anything to escape from his company. There was something happening between them and she felt frightened and confused and excited, all at the same time.

The basketball hoop was positioned above the garage door at the end of the long driveway. Pat was attending the University of Washington with the express hope of making the Husky basketball team. His whole life revolved around the game. He was rarely seen without a ball tucked under his arm and sometimes Ellen wondered if he showered with it. Or if the ball was glued to his armpit. She was well aware that the invitation to practice a few free throws with him was not meant to be taken literally. The only slam dunk Ellen had ever accomplished was with a doughnut in her hot chocolate. Her main job was to stand on the sidelines and be awed by Pat's talent. He needed someone to look upon him with appreciative eyes now and then and she fulfilled the role admirably.

They hadn't been in the driveway fifteen minutes when the back door opened and Derek strolled out, his forehead contracted in a tight frown. "Say, Ellen, have you got a minute?"

"What's your problem, my friend?"

"It's Michelle."

Lowering himself onto the concrete porch step, Derek gazed at Ellen with those wide pleading eyes of his.

Ellen sat beside him and wrapped her arms around her bent knees. "What's wrong with Michelle?"

"Nothing. She's beautiful and I think she may even fall in love with me, given the chance." He paused to sigh expressively. "I asked her out to dinner tonight."

"Naturally she agreed. Right?" If Michelle was anywhere near as taken with Derek as he was with her, she wasn't likely to refuse.

The boyishly thin shoulders heaved in a gesture of despair. "She can't."

"Why not?" Ellen watched as Pat bounced the basketball across the driveway, pivoted, jumped high in the air and sent the ball swooshing through the net.

"Apparently Michelle promised her older sister that she'd baby-sit tonight."

"That's too bad." Ellen gave him a sympathetic look.

"The thing is, she'd probably go out with me if there was someone who'd be willing to watch her niece and nephew for her. It has to be an adult so that Michelle wouldn't worry about them."

"That sounds reasonable." Pat made another skillful play and Ellen applauded vigorously. He rewarded her with a triumphant smile.

"Then you will?"

Ellen switched her attention from Pat's antics at the basketball hoop back to Derek. "Will I what?"

"Baby-sit Michelle's niece and nephew?"

"What?" she nearly exploded. "Not me. I've got to do the research for a term paper."

"Ellen, please, please, please."

"No. No. No." She sliced the air forcefully with her hand and jumped to her feet.

Derek rose with her. "I sense some resistance to this idea."

"The boy's a wonder," she mumbled under her breath as she hurried into the kitchen. "I've got to write my term paper. You know that."

Derek followed her inside. "Ellen, please. I promise I'll never ask anything of you again."

"I've heard that before." She tried to ignore him as he trailed her to the refrigerator and watched her take out sandwich makings for lunch.

"It's a matter of utter importance," Derek pleaded anew.

"What is?" Reed spoke from behind the morning paper he was reading at the kitchen table.

"This date with Michelle. Listen, Ellen, I bet Reed would help you. You're not doing anything tonight, are you?"

Reed lowered the newspaper. "Help Ellen with what?"

"Baby-sitting."

Reed glanced from the intent expression on his younger brother's face to the stubborn look on Ellen's. "You two leave me out of this."

"Ellen. Dear, sweet Ellen, you've got to understand that it could be weeks—weeks," he repeated dramatically, "before Michelle will be free to go out with me again."

Ellen plunked down an armload of cheese, ham and assorted jars of mustard and pickles. "*No!* Can I make it any plainer than that? I'm sorry, Derek, honest. But I can't."

"Reed," Derek pleaded with his brother. "Say something that will convince her."

"I'm out of this one."

He raised the newspaper again, but Ellen could sense a smile hidden behind it. Still, she doubted that Reed would be foolish enough to involve himself in the proceedings.

"Ellen, puleease."

"No." Ellen realized that if she wanted any peace, she'd have to forget about lunch and make an immediate escape. She whirled around and headed out of the kitchen, the door swinging in her wake.

"I think she's weakening," she heard Derek say as he followed her.

She was on her way up the stairs when she caught sight of Derek in the formal dining room, coming toward her on his knees, his hands folded in supplication. "Won't you please reconsider?"

Ellen groaned. "What do I need to say to convince you? I've got to get to the library. That paper is due Monday morning."

"I'll write it for you."

"No, thanks."

At just that moment Reed came through the door. "It shouldn't be too difficult to find a reliable teenager.

There are a few families with teenagers living in the neighborhood, as I recall.''

''I . . . don't know,'' Derek hedged.

''If we can't find anyone, then Danielle and I'll manage. It'll be good practice for us. Besides, just how much trouble can two kids be?''

When she heard that, Ellen had to swallow a burst of laughter. Reed obviously hadn't spent much time around children, she thought with a mischievous grin.

''How old did you say these kids are?'' She couldn't resist asking.

''Nine and four.'' Derek's dark eyes brightened expectantly as he leaped to his feet and gave his brother a grateful smile. ''So I can tell Michelle everything's taken care of?''

''I suppose.'' Reed's gaze sought out Ellen. ''I was young once myself,'' he said pointedly, reminding her of the comment she'd made the night before.

''I really appreciate this, Reed. I'll be your slave for life. I'd even loan you money if I had some. By the way, can I borrow your car tonight?''

''Don't press your luck.''

''Right.'' Derek chuckled, bounding up the stairs.

THE DOORBELL CHIMED close to six o'clock, just as Ellen was gathering up her books and preparing to leave for the library.

''That'll be Michelle,'' Derek called excitedly. ''Can you get it, Ellen?''

''No problem.''

Coloring books and crayons were arranged on the coffee table, along with some building blocks that Reed must have gone out and purchased that afternoon. From bits and pieces of information she'd picked up, she concluded that Reed had discovered it wasn't quite as easy to find a teenage baby-sitter as he'd assumed. And with no other recourse, he and Danielle were apparently taking over the task. Ellen wished him luck, but she really did need to concentrate on this stupid term paper. Reed hadn't suggested that Ellen wait around to meet Danielle and Ellen hadn't offered. But she had to admit she'd been wondering about the woman from the time Derek had first mentioned her.

"Hello, Ellen." Blond Michelle greeted Ellen with a warm, eager smile. They'd met briefly the other night. "This sure is great of Derek's brother and girlfriend, isn't it?"

"It sure is."

The four-year-old boy was clinging to Michelle's pant leg so that her gait was stiff-kneed as she loped into the house with the child attached to her thigh.

"Jimmy, this is Ellen. You'll be staying in her house tonight while Auntie Michelle goes out to dinner with Derek."

"I want my mommy."

"He won't be a problem," Michelle told Ellen confidently.

"I thought there were two children."

"Yeah, the baby's in the car. I'll be right back."

"Baby?" Ellen swallowed down a laugh. "What baby?"

"Jenny's nine months."

"Nine months?" A small uncontrollable giggle slid from her throat. This would be marvelous. Reed with a nine-month-old was almost too good to miss.

"Jimmy, you stay here." Somehow Michelle was able to pry the four-year-old's fingers loose from her leg and pass the struggling child to Ellen.

Kicking and thrashing, Jimmy broke into loud sobs as Ellen carried him into the living room. "Here's a coloring book. Do you like to color, Jimmy?"

But he refused to talk to Ellen or even look at her, as he buried his face in the sofa cushions. "I want my mommy," he wailed again.

By the time Michelle had returned with a baby carrier and a fussing nine-month-old, Derek sauntered suavely out from the kitchen. "Hey, Michelle, you're looking good."

Reed, who was following closely behind, came to a shocked standstill when he saw the baby. "I thought you said they were nine and four."

"I did," Derek explained patiently, his eyes devouring the blonde at his side.

"They won't be any trouble," Michelle cooed as Derek placed an arm around her shoulders and led her toward the open door.

"Derek, we need to talk," Reed insisted, his voice tinged with exasperation.

"Haven't got time now. I made our reservations for seven." His hand slid from Michelle's shoulders to her waist. "I'm taking my lady out for a night on the town."

"Derek," Reed demanded.

"Oh," Michelle tore her gaze from Derek's. "The diaper bag is in the entryway. Jenny should be dry, but you might want to check her later. She'll probably cry for a few minutes once she notices I'm gone, but that'll stop almost immediately."

Reed's face was grim as he cast a speculative glance toward Jimmy, who was still howling for his mother. The happily gurgling Jenny looked up at the unfamiliar dark-haired man and noticed for the first time that she was at the mercy of a stranger. She immediately burst into heart-wrenching tears.

"I want my mommy," Jimmy demanded yet again.

"I can see you've got everything under control," Ellen announced, reaching for her coat. "I'm sure Danielle will be here any minute."

"Ellen..."

"Don't expect me back soon. I've got hours of research ahead of me."

"You aren't really going to leave, are you?" Reed gave her a horrified look.

"I wish I could stay," she lied breezily. "Another time, maybe." With that, she was out the door, smiling as she bounded down the stairs.

CHAPTER THREE

AN UNEASY FEELING struck Ellen as she stood waiting at the bus stop. But she resolutely hardened herself against the impulse to rush right back to Reed and his disconsolate charges. Danielle would show up at any minute and Ellen really was obliged to do the research for her yet-to-be-determined math paper. Besides, she reminded herself, Reed had volunteered to baby-sit and she wasn't responsible for rescuing him. But those marvelous eyes of his had pleaded with her so earnestly. Ellen felt herself beginning to weaken. *No!* she mumbled under her breath. Reed had Danielle, and as far as Ellen was concerned, they were on their own.

However, by the time she arrived at the undergraduate library, Ellen discovered that she couldn't get Reed's pleading look out of her mind. From everything she'd heard about Danielle, Ellen realized the woman probably didn't know the first thing about babies. As for the term paper, she supposed she could put it off until Sunday. After all, she'd looked for excuses all day to avoid working on it. She'd done the wash, trimmed the shrubs, cleaned the downspouts and washed the upstairs walls in an effort to escape that paper. One more night wasn't going to make much difference.

Hurriedly, she signed out some books and journals that looked as though they might be helpful and headed for the bus stop. Ellen had to admit that she was curious enough to want to meet Danielle. Reed's girlfriend had to be someone very special to put up with his frequent absences—or else a schemer, as Derek had implied. But Ellen couldn't see Reed being duped by a woman, no matter how clever or sophisticated she might be.

Her speculations came to an end as the bus eased to a stop at the curb and Ellen quickly jumped on for the short ride home.

Reed was kneeling on the carpet changing the still-tearful Jenny's diaper when Ellen walked in the front door. He seemed to have aged ten years in the past hour. A diaper pin was clenched between his teeth and the long sleeves of his wool shirt were rolled up to the elbows.

Reed took one look at her and sagged with relief. "Thank God you're here. She hasn't stopped crying from the minute you left."

"You look like you're doing a good job without me. Where's Danielle?"

He muttered a few words of profanity under his breath. "She couldn't stay." He finished the diapering and awkwardly tugged the plastic pants back into place. "That wasn't so difficult," he said, glancing proudly at Ellen as he stood Jenny up on the floor, holding the baby upright by her small arms.

Ellen swallowed a laugh as she noticed the bunches of material sticking out from the legs and waist of Jenny's plastic pants. She was trying to think of a tactful way of pointing it out to Reed when both the diaper and the plastic pants began to slide down Jenny's pudgy legs, settling at her ankles.

"Maybe you should try," Reed conceded, handing her the baby. Within minutes, Ellen had successfully re-folded and secured the diaper. Unfortunately, she didn't manage to soothe the baby any more than Reed had.

Cradling Jenny in her arms, Ellen paced the area in front of the fireplace, at a loss to comfort the sobbing child. "I don't know that I'll do any better. It's been a while since my brother was this size."

"Women are always better at this kind of stuff," Reed argued, rubbing a hand over his face. "Most women," he amended, with such a look of frustration that Ellen smiled.

"I bet Jimmy knows what to do," she suggested next, pleased with her inspiration. The little boy might actually come up with something helpful, and involving him in their attempts to comfort Jenny might distract him from his own unhappiness. Or so Ellen hoped. "Jimmy's a good big brother. Isn't that right, honey?"

The child lifted his face from the sofa cushion. "I want my mommy."

"Let's pretend Ellen is your mommy," Reed offered.

"No! She's like that other lady who said bad words."

Meanwhile, Jenny wailed all the louder. Digging around in the diaper bag, Reed found a stuffed teddy bear and pressed it into her arms. But Jenny angrily tossed the toy aside, the tears flowing unabated down her face.

"Come on, Jimmy," Reed pleaded desperately into the din. "We need a little help here. Your sister is crying."

Holding his hands over his eyes, Jimmy straightened and peeked through two fingers. The distraught Jenny continued to cry at full volume in spite of Ellen's best efforts to comfort her.

"Mommy bounces her."

Ellen had been gently doing that from the beginning.

"What else?" she encouraged.

"She likes her boo-loo."

"What's that?"

"Her teddy bear."

"I've already tried that," Reed snorted. "What else does your mommy do when she cries like this?"

Jimmy was thoughtful for a moment. "Oh." The four-year-old's eyes sparkled. "Mommy nurses her."

Reed and Ellen glanced at each other and dissolved into giggles. The laughter faded from his eyes and was replaced with a roguish grin. "That could prove to be interesting."

Hiding a smile, Ellen decided to ignore Reed's comment. "Sorry, Jenny," she said softly to the baby girl, "but mine are strictly for decoration."

"But maybe he's got an idea," Reed suggested eagerly. "Could she be hungry?"

"It's worth a try. At this point, anything is."

Jenny's bellowing had finally dwindled into a few hiccupping sobs. And for some reason, Jimmy suddenly straightened and stared at Reed's craggy face, at his deep auburn hair and brilliant green eyes. Then he pointed to the plaid wool shirt, its long sleeves rolled up to the elbows. "Are you Paul Bunyan?"

"Paul Bunyan?" Reed repeated, looking puzzled. "You mean the lumberjack?" He broke into a full laugh. "No, but I imagine I must look like him to you."

Rummaging through the diaper bag, Ellen found a plastic bottle filled with milk. Jenny eyed it skeptically, but no sooner had Ellen removed the cap than Jenny grabbed it from her hands and began sucking eagerly at the nipple.

Sighing, Ellen sank into the rocking chair and gently swayed back and forth with the baby securely tucked in her arms. "I guess that settles that."

"Aren't you supposed to heat those things?"

"That's what I thought," Ellen agreed. The silence was so blissful that she wanted to wrap it around herself. She felt the tension drain from her muscles as she relaxed in the rocking chair. From tidbits Jimmy had dropped, she surmised that Danielle hadn't been much help. Everything she'd learned about the other woman told Ellen that Danielle would probably find young children frustrating—and apparently she had.

Jimmy had crawled into Reed's lap with a book and demanded that Paul Bunyan read to him. Together the two leafed through the colorful storybook. Several times during the peaceful interlude, Ellen's eyes met Reed's across the room and they exchanged a contented smile.

Jenny sucked tranquilly at the bottle, and her eyes slowly drooped shut. At peace with her world, the baby was utterly satisfied to be tenderly held and rocked to sleep. Ellen gazed down at the angelic face, and brushed fine wisps of hair from the untroubled forehead. Releasing her breath in a slow, drawn-out sigh, she glanced up to discover Reed watching her, the little boy still sitting quietly on his lap.

"Well, Mother Ellen, you've finally got a baby in your arms," he said softly.

"I guess I do, at that."

"Ellen?" Reed spoke in a low voice. "Did you finish your math paper?"

"Finish it?" She groaned. "Are you kidding? I haven't even started it."

"What's a math paper?" Jimmy asked curiously.

Gently rocking the baby, Ellen looked solemnly over at the boy. "Well, it's something I have to write for a math class. And if I don't write a paper, I haven't got even a hope of passing the course." She didn't think he'd understand any algebraic terms. For that matter, neither did she.

"What's math?"

"Numbers," Reed told the boy.

"And, in this case, sometimes letters—like x and y."

"I like numbers," Jimmy declared proudly. "I like three and nine and seven."

"Well, Jimmy, my boy, how would you like to write my paper for me?"

"Can I?"

Ellen was more than willing to transfer the task. "You bet."

Reed got out pencil and paper and set the four-year-old to work.

Glancing up, she gave Reed a soft smile. "See how easy this is? You're good with kids." Reed grinned at her in answer as he carefully drew numbers for Jimmy to copy.

After several minutes of this activity, Jimmy decided it was time to put on his pajamas. Seeing him yawn, Reed brought down a pillow and blanket and tucked him into a hastily made bed on the sofa. Then he read a bedtime story until the four-year-old again yawned loudly and cuddled into a tight ball.

Ellen still hadn't moved, fearing that the slightest jolt would rouse the baby.

"Why don't we set her down in the baby seat?" Reed prompted.

"I'm afraid she'll wake."

"If she does, you can rock her again."

His suggestion made sense and besides, her arms were beginning to ache. "Okay." He moved to her side and gently lifted the sleeping child. Ellen flexed her muscles, unaccustomed to holding them in one position for so long. She held her breath momentarily when Jenny stirred. But the little girl simply rolled her head against the cushion and returned to sleep.

Ellen rose to her feet and turned the lamp down to its dimmest setting, surrounding them with a warm circle of light.

"I couldn't have done it without you," Reed whispered, coming to stand beside her. He rested his hand at the back of her neck.

An unfamiliar warmth seeped through Ellen, and she began to talk quickly, hoping to conceal her sudden nervousness. "Sure you could have. From my point of view, you had everything under control."

Reed snorted. "I was ten minutes away from calling the crisis clinic. Thanks for coming to the rescue." He casually withdrew his hand, and Ellen felt both relieved and disappointed.

"You're welcome." She was dying to know what had happened with Danielle, but she didn't want to ask. Apparently, the other woman hadn't stayed around for too long.

"Have you eaten?"

Ellen had been so busy that she'd forgotten about dinner, but once Reed mentioned it, she realized how hungry she was. "No, and I'm starved."

"Do you like Chinese food?"

"Love it."

"Good. There's enough for an army out in the kitchen. I ordered it earlier."

Ellen didn't need to be told that he'd made dinner plans with Danielle in mind. He'd expected to share an intimate candle-lit evening with her. "Listen," she began awkwardly, clasping her hands in front of her. "I really have to get going on this term paper. Why don't you call Danielle and invite her back? Now that the kids are asleep, I'm sure everything will be better. I—"

"Children make Danielle nervous. She warned me about it, but I refused to listen. She's home now and has probably taken some aspirin and gone to sleep. I can't see letting good food go to waste. Besides, it gives me an opportunity to thank you."

"Oh." It was the longest speech that Reed had made. "All right," she agreed with a slight nod.

While Reed warmed the food in the microwave, Ellen set out plates and forks and brewed a large pot of tea, placing it in the middle of the table. The swinging door that connected the kitchen with the living room was left open in case either child awoke.

"What do we need plates for?" Reed asked with a questioning arch of his brow.

"Plates are the customary eating device."

"Not tonight."

"Not tonight?" Something dark and amusing glinted in Reed's eyes as he set out several white boxes and brandished two pairs of chopsticks. "Since it's only the two of us, we can eat right out of the boxes."

"I'm not very adept with chopsticks." The smell drifting from the open boxes was tangy and enticing.

"You'll learn if you're hungry."

"I'm starved."

"Good." Deftly he took the first pair of chopsticks and showed her how to work them with her thumb and index finger.

Imitating his movements Ellen discovered that her fingers weren't nearly as agile as his. Two or three tries at picking up small pieces of spicy diced chicken succeeded only in frustrating her.

"Here." Reed fed her a bite from the end of his chop-sticks. "Be a little more patient with yourself."

"That's easy for you to say while you're eating your fill and I'm starving to death."

"It'll come."

Ellen grumbled under her breath, but a few tries later she managed to deliver a portion of the hot food to her eager mouth.

"See, I told you you'd pick this up fast enough."

"Do you always tell someone 'I told you so'?" she asked with pretended annoyance. The mood was too congenial for any real discontent. Ellen felt that they'd shared a special time together looking after the two small children. More than special—astonishing. They hadn't clashed once or found a single thing to squabble over.

"I enjoy teasing you. Your eyes have an irresistible way of lighting up when you're angry."

"If you continue to insist that I eat with these absurd pieces of wood, you'll see my eyes brighten the entire room."

"I'm looking forward to that," he murmured with a soft laugh. "No forks. You can't properly enjoy Chinese food unless you use chopsticks."

"I can't properly *taste* it without a fork."

"Here, I'll feed you." Again he brought a spicy morsel to her mouth.

A drop of the juice bounced against her chin and Ellen wiped it off. "You aren't any better than me." She dipped the chopsticks into the chicken mixture and attempted to transport a tidbit to Reed's mouth. The small piece of white meat balanced precariously on the end of the chopsticks, and Reed lowered his mouth to catch it before it could land in his lap.

"You're improving," he told her, his voice low and slightly husky.

Their eyes met. Unable to face the caressing look in his warm gaze, Ellen bent her head and pretended to be engrossed in her dinner. But her appetite was instantly gone—vanished.

A tense silence filled the room. The air between them was so charged that she felt breathless and weak, as though she'd lost the energy to move or speak. Ellen didn't dare raise her eyes for fear of what she'd see in his.

"Ellen."

She took a deep breath and scrambled to her feet, battling down the frantic beating of her heart. "I think I hear Jimmy," she whispered.

"Maybe it was Jenny," Reed added hurriedly.

Ellen paused in the doorway between the two rooms. They were both overwhelmingly aware that neither child had made a sound. "I think they're still asleep."

"That's good." The scraping sound of his chair against the floor told her that Reed, too, had risen from the table. When she turned, she found him depositing the leftovers from their dinner in the refrigerator. His preoccupation with the task gave her a moment to reflect on what had just happened. There were too many problems involved in pursuing this attraction and they both knew it. The best thing to do was ignore it and hope the craziness passed. They were mature adults, not adolescents, and besides, this would complicate her life, which was something she didn't need right now. Neither, she was sure, did he.

"If you don't mind, I think I'll head upstairs," she began awkwardly, taking a step in retreat.

"That shouldn't be a problem. I appreciated the help."

"I appreciated the dinner," she returned.

"I'll see you in the morning then."

"Right." Neither seemed eager to bring the evening to an end.

"Good night, Ellen."

"Night, Reed. Call if you need me."

"I will."

Turning decisively, she took the stairs and was panting by the time she'd climbed up the second narrow flight. The third floor had originally been built to accommodate servants. The five bedrooms were small and opened onto a large central room, which was where Ellen had placed her bed. She'd chosen the largest of the bedrooms as her study.

She sat resolutely down at her desk and leafed frantically through several books, hoping to come across an idea she could use for her term paper. But her thoughts were dominated by the man two floors below. Clutching a study on the origins of algebra to her chest, she sighed deeply and wondered whether Danielle truly appreciated Reed. She must. Few women would be so willing to sit at home waiting, while their fiancés traipsed around the world directing a variety of projects.

Reed had been so patient and good-natured with Jimmy and little Jenny. When the youngster had climbed into his lap, Reed had read to him and held him with a tenderness that stirred her heart. And Reed was generous to a fault. Any other man would have told Pat, Monte and Ellen to pack their bags. This was his home, after all, and Derek had been wrong to rent out the rooms without Reed's knowledge. But Reed had let them stay.

Disgruntled with the trend her thoughts were taking, Ellen forced her mind back to the books in front of her. But it wasn't long before her concentration started to drift again. Reed had Danielle, and she had . . . Charlie

Hanson. First thing in the morning, she'd call good old dependable Charlie and suggest they get together; he'd probably be as surprised as he was pleased to hear from her. Feeling relieved and a little light-headed, Ellen turned off the light and went to bed.

"WHAT ARE YOU DOING?" Reed arrived in the kitchen early the next afternoon, looking as though he'd just finished eighteen holes of golf or a vigorous game of tennis. He glowed with health and vitality. Reed had already left by the time she'd wandered down to the kitchen that morning.

"Ellen?" he repeated impatiently.

The wall plates were off the electrical outlets and the receptacle had been pulled out of its box, from which two thin colored wires, now protruded. "I'm trying to figure out why this outlet won't heat the iron," she answered without looking in his direction.

"You're what!" he bellowed.

She wiped her face to remove a layer of dust before she straightened. "Don't yell at me."

"Good grief, woman. You run around on the roof like a trapeze artist, cook like a dream and do electrical work on the side. Is there anything you can't do?"

"Algebra," she muttered.

Reed closed the instruction manual Ellen had propped against the sugar bowl in the middle of the table. He took her by the shoulders and pushed her gently aside, then reattached the electrical wires and fastened the whole thing back in place.

As he finished securing the wall plate, Ellen burst out, "What did you do that for? I've almost got the problem traced."

"No doubt, but if you don't mind, I'd rather have a real electrician look at this."

"What can I say? It's your house."

"Right. Now sit down." He nudged her into a chair. "How much longer are you going to delay writing that term paper?"

"It's written," she snapped. She wasn't particularly pleased with it, but at least the assignment was done. Her subject matter might impress four-year-old Jimmy, but she wasn't too confident that her professor would appreciate her effort.

"Do you want me to look it over?"

The offer surprised her. "No, thanks." She stuck the screwdriver in the pocket of her gray-striped coveralls.

"Well, that wasn't so hard, was it?"

"I just don't think I've got a snowball's chance of getting a decent grade on it. Anyway, I have to go and iron a dress. I've got a date."

A dark brow lifted over inscrutable green eyes and he seemed about to say something.

"Reed." Unexpectedly, the kitchen door swung open and a soft, feminine voice purred his name. "What's taking you so long?"

"Danielle, I'd like you to meet Ellen."

"Hello." Ellen resisted the urge to kick Reed. If he was going to introduce her to his friend, the least he could have done was waited until she looked a little more presentable. Just as she'd figured, Danielle was beautiful. No, the word was gorgeous. She wore a cute pale-blue one-piece outfit with a short, pleated skirt. A dark-blue silk scarf held back the curly cascade of long blond hair—Ellen should have known the other woman would be blond. Naturally, Danielle possessed a trim waist, perfect legs and blue eyes to match the heavens. She'd apparently just finished playing golf or tennis with Reed, but she still looked cool and elegant.

"I feel as though I already know you," Danielle was saying with a pleasant smile. "Reed told me how much of a help you were with the children."

"It was nothing, really." Embarrassed by her ridiculous outfit, Ellen tried to conceal as much of it as possible by grabbing the electrical repair book and clasping it to her stomach.

"Not according to Reed." Danielle slipped her arm around his and smiled adoringly up at him. "Unfortunately, I came down with a terrible headache."

"Danielle doesn't have your knack with young children," Reed inserted.

"If we decide to have our own, things will be different," Danielle continued sweetly. "But I'm not convinced I'm the motherly type."

Taking a step backward, Ellen offered the couple a wan smile. "If you'll excuse me, I've got to change my clothes."

"Of course. It was nice meeting you, Elaine."

"Ellen," Reed and Ellen corrected simultaneously.

"You, too." Gallantly, Ellen stifled the childish impulse to call the other woman Diane. As she turned and headed up the narrow stairs leading from the kitchen, she heard Danielle whisper that she didn't mind in the least if Ellen lived in Reed's home. Of course not, Ellen muttered to herself. How could Danielle possibly be jealous?

Winded by the time she'd marched up both flights, Ellen walked into the tiny bedroom where she stored her clothes. She slammed down the electrical manual and kicked the door shut with her foot. Then she sighed with anger and frustration as she saw her reflection in the full-length mirror on the back of the door; it revealed baggy coveralls, a faded white T-shirt and smudges of dirt across her cheekbone. She struck a seductive pose with her hand on her hip and vampishly puffed up her hair. "Of course, I don't mind if sweet little Elaine lives here, darling," she mimicked in a high-pitched falsely sweet voice.

Dropping her coveralls to the ground, Ellen gruffly kicked them aside. Hands on her hips, she glared at her reflection. Her figure was no less attractive than Danielle's, and her face was pretty enough—even if she did say so herself. But Danielle had barely looked at Ellen and certainly hadn't seen her as a potential rival. That was what frustrated Ellen most.

As she brushed her hair away from her face, Ellen's shoulders suddenly dropped. She was losing her mind! She liked living with the boys. Their arrangement was ideal, yet here she was, complaining bitterly because her presence hadn't been challenged.

Carefully choosing her light-pink blouse and matching maroon skirt, Ellen told herself that Charlie, at least, would appreciate her. And for now, Ellen needed that. Her self-confidence had been shaken by Danielle's casual acceptance of her role in Reed's house. She didn't like Danielle. But then, she hadn't expected to.

"ELLEN." Her name was followed by a loud pounding on the bedroom door. "Wake up! There's a phone call for you."

"Okay," she mumbled into her pillow, still caught in the last dregs of sleep. It felt so warm and cozy under the thick blankets that she didn't want to stir. Charlie had taken her to dinner and a movie and they'd returned a little after ten. The boys had stayed in that evening, but

Reed was out and Ellen didn't need to ask with whom. She hadn't heard him come home.

"Ellen."

"I'm awake, I'm awake," she grumbled, slipping one leg free of the covers, and dangling it over the edge of the bed. The sudden cold that assailed her bare foot made her eyes flutter open in momentary shock.

"It sounds long distance."

Her eyes did open then. She knew only one person who could be calling. Her mother!

Hurriedly tossing the covers aside, she grabbed her housecoat and scurried out of the room. "Why didn't you tell me it was long distance before now?"

"I tried," Pat complained. "But you were more interested in sleeping."

A glance at her clock radio told her it was barely seven.

Taking a deep, calming breath, Ellen walked quickly down one flight of stairs and picked up the telephone receiver at the end of the hallway.

"Good morning, Mom."

"How'd you know it was me?" came the soft, familiar voice.

Although they wrote to each other regularly, this was the first time her mother had actually phoned her since she'd left home. "Lucky guess."

"Who was that young man who answered the phone?"

"Patrick."

"The basketball kid."

Her mother had read every word of her letters. "That's him."

"Has Monte eaten you out of house and home yet?"

"Just about."

"And has this Derek kid finally summoned up enough nerve to ask out . . . what was her name again?"

"Michelle."

"Right. That's the one."

"They saw each other twice this weekend," Ellen told her, feeling a sharp pang of homesickness.

"And what about you, Ellen? Are you dating?" It wasn't an idle question. Through the years, Ellen's mother had often fretted that her oldest child was giving up her youth in order to care for the family. Ellen didn't deny that she'd made sacrifices, but they'd been willing ones.

Her letters home had been chatty, but she hadn't mentioned Charlie, and Ellen wasn't sure whether she wanted her mother to know about him. Her relationship with him was based on friendship and nothing more, although Ellen suspected that Charlie would have liked it to develop into something romantic.

"Mom, you didn't phone me long distance on a Monday morning to discuss my social life."

"You're right. I called to discuss mine."

"And?" Ellen's heart hammered against her ribs. Already she knew what was coming. She'd known it months ago, even before she moved to Seattle. Her mother was going to remarry. After ten years of widowhood, Dorothy Cunningham had found another man to love.

"And—" her mother faltered "—James has asked me to be his wife."

"And?" It seemed to Ellen that her vocabulary had suddenly been reduced to one word.

"And I've said yes."

Ellen closed her eyes, expecting to feel a rush of bittersweet nostalgia for the father she remembered so well and loved so much. Instead, she felt only gladness that her mother had found another happiness.

"Congratulations, Mom."

"Do you mean that?"

"With all my heart. When's the wedding?"

"Well, actually..." Her mother hedged again. "Honey, don't be angry."

"Angry?"

"We're already married. I'm calling from Reno."

"Oh."

"Are you mad?"

"Of course not."

"James has a winter home in Arizona and we're going to honeymoon here until April."

"April," Ellen repeated, sounding a little dazed.

"If you object, honey, I'll come back to Yakima for Christmas."

"No...I don't object. It's just a little sudden."

"Dad's been gone ten years."

"I know, Mom. Don't you worry."

"I'll write soon."

"Do that. And much happiness, Mom. You and James deserve it."

"Thank you, love."

They spoke for a few more minutes before saying goodbye. Ellen walked down the stairs in a state of stunned disbelief, absentmindedly tightening the belt of her housecoat. In a matter of months, her entire family had disintegrated. Her sister and mother had married and Bud had joined the service.

"Good morning," she cautiously greeted Reed, who was sitting at the kitchen table already dressed and reading the paper.

"Morning," he responded dryly, as he lowered his newspaper.

Her hands trembling, Ellen reached for a mug, but it slipped out of her fingers and hit the counter, luckily without breaking.

Reed carefully folded the newspaper and studied her face. "What's wrong? You look like you've just seen a ghost."

"My mom's married."

"Why the fuss? That should remove an ugly mark from your birth certificate."

"It's not my father."

"Ah, the plot thickens."

"Stop it, Reed," she murmured in a subdued voice. Tears burned in her eyes. She was no longer sure just what she was feeling. Happiness for her mother, yes, but also sadness as she remembered her father and his untimely death.

"You're serious."

"I'm afraid so." She sat across from him at the table, holding the mug in both hands and staring into its depths. "It isn't like it's sudden. Dad's been gone a lot of years. What surprises me is all the emotion I'm feeling."

"That's only natural. I remember how I felt when my dad remarried. I'd known for months that Mary and Dad were going to marry. But the day of the wedding I felt that my father had betrayed the memory of my mother. Those were heavy thoughts for a ten-year-old boy." His hand gently reached for hers. "As I recall, that was the last time I cried."

The emotion filled her eyes and Ellen nodded. It was the only way she could thank him, because speaking was impossible, just then. She knew instinctively that Reed didn't often share the hurts of his youth.

Just when her throat had relaxed and she felt she could speak, Derek threw open the back door and dashed in, tossing his older brother a set of keys.

"I had them add a quart of oil," Derek said. "Are you sure you can't stay longer?"

The sip of coffee sank to the pit of Ellen's stomach and sat there. "You're leaving?" Suddenly she felt as though someone had jerked her chair out from under her.

He released her hand and gave it a gentle pat. "You'll be fine."

Ellen forced her concentration back to the black coffee. For days she'd been telling herself that she'd be relieved and delighted when Reed left. Now she dreaded it. More than anything, she wanted him to stay.

CHAPTER FOUR

"ELLEN," DEREK SHOUTED as he burst in the front door, his hands full of mail. "Can I invite Michelle to dinner Friday night?"

Casually, Ellen looked up from the textbook she was studying. By mutual agreement, they all went their separate ways on Friday evenings and Ellen didn't cook. If one of the boys happened to be in the house, he heated up soup or put together a thick sandwich or made do with leftovers. In Monte's case, he did all three.

"What are you planning to fix?" Ellen responded cagily.

"Cook? Me?" Derek slapped his hand against his chest and looked utterly shocked. "I can't cook. You know that."

"But you're inviting company."

His gaze dropped and he restlessly shuffled his feet. "I was hoping that maybe this one Friday you could..." He paused and his head jerked up. "You don't have a date, do you?" He sounded as though that was the worst possible thing that could happen.

"Not this Friday."

"Oh, good. For a minute there, I thought we might have a problem."

"We?" She arched her brows playfully. "I don't have a problem, but it sounds like you do." She wasn't going to let him con her into his schemes quite so easily.

"But you'll be here."

"I was planning on soaking in the tub, giving my hair a hot-oil treatment and hibernating with a good book." Her gaze fell on the algebra text and she involuntarily grimaced.

"But you could still fix dinner, couldn't you? Something simple like seafood jambalaya with shrimp, stuffed eggplant and pecan pie for dessert."

"Are you planning to rob a bank as well?" At his blank stare, she elaborated. "Honestly, Derek, have you checked out the price of seafood lately?"

"No, but you cooked that Cajun meal not so long ago and—"

"Shrimp was on sale," she broke in.

He continued undaunted. "And it was probably the most delicious meal I've ever tasted in my whole life. I was kicking myself because Reed wasn't here and he would have loved it as much as everyone else."

At the mention of Reed's name, Ellen's lashes fell, hiding the confusion and longing in her eyes. The house had been full of college boys and their shenanigans, yet it had seemed astonishingly empty without Reed. He'd been with them barely a week and Ellen couldn't believe how much his presence had affected her. The morning he'd left, she'd walked him out to the truck, trying to think of a way to say goodbye and to thank him for understanding the emotions that raged through her at the news of her mother's marriage. But nothing had turned out quite as she'd expected. Reed had seemed just as reluctant to say goodbye as she was, and before climbing inside the truck, he'd leaned forward and lightly brushed his lips over hers. The kiss had been so spontaneous that Ellen wasn't sure if he'd really meant to do it. But intentional or not, he *had*, and the memory of that kiss stayed with her. Now a day rarely passed that he didn't enter her thoughts, one way or another.

A couple of times when she was on the second floor she'd wandered into her old bedroom, forgetting that it now belonged to Reed. Both times, she'd lingered there, enjoying the sensation of remembering Reed and their verbal battles.

Repeatedly Ellen told herself that it was because Derek's brother was over twenty-one and she could therefore carry on an adult conversation with him. Although she was genuinely fond of the boys, she'd discovered that a constant diet of their antics and their adolescent preoccupations—Pat's basketball, Monte's appetite and Derek's Michelle—didn't exactly make for stimulating conversation.

"You really are a fantastic cook," Derek went on. "Even better than my mother. Why, only the other day Monte was saying..."

"Don't you think you're putting it on a little thick, Derek? If you continue like this, I may be forced to walk around in hip boots."

The teenager blinked twice. "I just wanted you to know how much I'd appreciate it if you did happen to decide to do me this tiny favor."

"You'll buy the ingredients yourself?"

"The grocery budget couldn't manage it this once?"

"Not unless everyone else is willing to eat oatmeal three times a week for the remainder of the month."

"I don't suppose they would be," he muttered. "All right, make me a list and I'll buy what you need."

Ellen was half hoping that once he saw the price of fresh shrimp, he'd realize it would be cheaper to take Michelle to a seafood restaurant.

"Oh, by the way," Derek said, examining one of the envelopes in his hand. "You got a letter. It looks like it's from Reed."

"Reed?" Her lungs slowly contracted as she said his name and it was all she could do not to snatch the envelope out of Derek's hand. The instant he gave it to her, she tore it open.

"What does he say?" Derek asked, sorting through the rest of the mail. "He didn't write me."

Ellen quickly scanned the contents. "He's asking if the electrician has come yet. That's all."

"Oh?"

She made a show of tucking the letter back inside the envelope. "I'll go into the kitchen and make that list for you before I forget."

"I appreciate it, Ellen, honest."

"Sure," she grumbled.

As soon as the kitchen door swung closed, Ellen took out Reed's letter again, intent on savoring every word.

Dear Ellen,
You're right, the Monterey area is beautiful. I wish I could say that everything else is as peaceful as the scenery here. Unfortunately it's not. Things have been hectic. But if all goes well, I should be back at the house by Saturday, which is earlier than I expected.

Have you become accustomed to the idea that your mother's remarried? I know it was a shock. I remember how I felt, and that was many years ago. I've been thinking about it all—and wondering about you. If I'd known what was happening, I might have been able to postpone this trip. You looked like you needed someone. And knowing you, it isn't often you're willing to lean on anyone. Not the independent, self-sufficient woman I discovered walking around half naked in my kitchen. I can almost see your face getting red when you read that. I shouldn't tease you, but I can't help it.

By the way, I contacted a friend of mine who owns an electrical business and told him the problem with the kitchen outlet. He said he'd try to stop by soon. He'll call first.

I'm not good at writing letters, but I wanted you to know that I was thinking about you and the boys. Actually, I'm pleased you're there to keep those kids in line. I know I came at you like a wounded bear when I first learned you were living in the house. I didn't mean to insult you. Derek is right, you're not that kind of woman. Problem is, I'm not sure what kind of woman you are. I've never known anyone quite like you.

Anyway, the electrician is coming, as promised. Take care and I'll see you late Saturday.

Say hi to the boys for me. I'm trusting that they aren't giving you any problems.

                                                    Reed

Ellen folded the letter and slipped it into her pocket. She crossed her arms, smiling to herself, feeling incredibly good. So Reed had been thinking about her. And she'd bet it was more than the troublesome kitchen outlet that had prompted his letter. Although she acknowledged that it would be dangerous for her to read too much into Reed's simple message, Ellen couldn't help but feel encouraged.

Humming softly, she propped open her cookbook, compiling the list of items Derek would need for his fancy dinner with Michelle. A few minutes later, her spirits soared still higher when the electrical contractor phoned and arranged a date and time to check the faulty outlet. Somehow, that seemed like a good omen to her—a kind of proof that she really was in Reed's thoughts.

"Was the phone for me?" Derek called from halfway down the staircase.

Ellen finished writing the information on the pad by the phone before answering. "It was the electrician Reed wrote about."

"Oh. I'm half expecting a call from Michelle."

"Speaking of your true love, here's your grocery list."

Derek took it and slowly ran his finger down the items she'd need for his special dinner with Michelle. "Is this going to cost over ten dollars?" He glanced up, his face doubtful.

"The pecans alone will be that much," she exaggerated.

With only a hint of disappointment, Derek shook his head. "I think maybe Michelle and I should find a nice, cosy, inexpensive restaurant."

Satisfied that her plan had worked so well, Ellen hid a smile. "I thought as much. By the way," she added, "Reed says he'll be home Saturday."

"So soon? He hasn't even been gone two weeks."

"Apparently it's only a short job."

"Apparently," Derek grumbled. "I don't have to be here, do I? Michelle wanted me to help her and her sister paint."

"Derek, my boy," Ellen said softly. "I didn't know you could wield a brush. The upstairs hallway—"

"Forget it," he told her sharply. "I'm only doing this to help Michelle."

"Right, but I bet Michelle would be willing to help you, since you're being so generous with your time."

"No way," he argued disgustedly. "We're college kids, not slaves."

The following afternoon, the electrician arrived and was in and out of the house within thirty minutes. Ellen felt proud that she'd correctly traced the problem. She could probably have fixed it if Reed hadn't become so frantic at the thought of her fumbling around with the kitchen wiring. Recalling his reaction produced an involuntary smile.

THAT EVENING, Ellen had finished loading the dishwasher and had just settled down at the kitchen table to study when the phone rang. Pat, who happened to be walking past the phone, answered it on the first ring.

"It's Reed," he told Ellen. "He wants to talk to you."

With reflexes that surprised even her, Ellen bounded out of her chair.

"Reed," she said into the telephone receiver, holding it tightly against her ear. "Hello, how are you?"

"Fine. Did the electrician come?"

"He was here this afternoon."

"Any problems?"

"No," she said breathily. He sounded wonderfully close, his voice warm and vibrant. "In fact, I was on the right track. I probably could have handled the problem myself."

"I don't want you to even think about fixing anything like that. You could end up killing yourself or someone else. I want you to understand that, Ellen. I absolutely forbid it."

"Aye, aye, sir." His words had the immediate effect of igniting her temper, sending the hot blood roaring through her veins. She hadn't been able to stop thinking about Reed since he'd left, but two minutes after picking up the phone, she was arguing with him again.

There was a long, awkward silence. Reed was the first to speak, expelling his breath sharply. "I didn't mean to snap your head off," he admitted.

"And I didn't mean to shout back," she answered, instantly soothed.

"How's everything else going?"

"Fine."

"Have the boys conned you into any more of their schemes?"

"They keep trying."

"They wouldn't be college kids if they didn't."

"I know." It piqued her a little that Reed assumed she could be bamboozled by three teenagers. "Don't worry about me. I can hold my own with these three."

His low sensuous chuckle did funny things to her pulse rate. "It's not you I'm concerned about."

"Just what are you implying?" she asked, a smile evident in her voice.

"I'm going to play this one smart and leave that last comment open-ended."

"Clever of you, my friend, very clever."

"I thought as much."

After a short pause, Ellen quickly asked, "How's everything your way?" She knew there really wasn't anything more to say, but she didn't want the conversation to end. Talking to Reed was almost as good as having him there.

"Much better, thanks. I shouldn't have any problem being home by Saturday."

"Good."

Another short silence followed.

"Well, I guess that's all I've got to say. If I'm going to be any later than Saturday, I'll give you a call."

"Drive carefully."

"I will. Bye, Ellen."

"Goodbye, Reed." Smiling, she replaced the receiver in its cradle. When she glanced up, all three boys were staring at her, their arms crossed dramatically over their chests.

"I think something's going on here," Pat spoke first. "I answered the phone and Reed asked for Ellen. He didn't even ask for Derek—his own brother."

"Right," Derek agreed. "Reed even wrote her a letter."

"I'm wondering," Monte said, rubbing his chin thoughtfully. "Could we have the makings of a romance on our hands?"

"I think we must," Pat concurred.

"Stop it." Ellen did her best to join in the banter, although she felt the color flooding her cheeks. "It's only natural that Reed would want to talk to me. I'm the oldest."

"But I'm his brother," Derek countered.

"I refuse to listen to any of this," she said with a small laugh and turned back to the kitchen. "You three aren't even making sense. Reed's dating Danielle."

All three followed her. "He could have married Danielle months ago if he was really interested," Derek informed the small gathering.

"Be still, my trembling heart," Monte joked, melodramatically folding both hands over his heart and pretending to swoon.

Not to be outdone, Pat placed the back of his hand against his forehead and rolled his eyes. "Ah, love."

"I'm getting out of here." Before anyone could argue, Ellen bounded up the back stairs to her room, laughing as she went. She had to admit she'd found the boys' little performances quite funny. But if they pulled any of their romance-brewing pranks around Reed, it would be extremely embarrassing for her. Ellen resolved to say something to them when the time seemed appropriate.

FRIDAY AFTERNOON, Ellen walked into the kitchen, her schoolbooks clutched tightly to her chest.

"What's the matter? You look pale as a ghost," Monte remarked, cramming a chocolate-chip cookie in his mouth.

Derek and Pat turned toward her, their faces revealing their concern.

"I got my algebra paper back today."

"And?" Derek prompted.

"I don't know. I haven't looked."

"Why not?"

"Because I know how tough ol' Engstrom was on the others. The girl who wrote about solving that oddball conjecture got a C-minus and the guy who was so enthusiastic about his subject of Mathematics in World War II got a D. With impressive subjects like that getting low grades, I'm doomed."

"But you worked hard on that paper." Loyally, Derek defended her and placed a consoling arm around her shoulders. "You found out a whole bunch of interesting facts about the number nine."

"You did your paper on that?" Pat asked, his smooth brow wrinkling with amusement.

"Don't laugh." She already felt enough of a fool.

"It isn't going to do any good to fret," Monte insisted with perfect logic, slipping the folded assignment from between her fingers.

Ellen watched his expression intently as he handed the paper to Derek who raised two thick brows and gave it to Pat.

"Well?"

"You got a B-minus," Pat said in a husky whisper, revealing his own surprise. "I don't believe it."

"Me neither." This was what heaven must feel like, Ellen decided, this delicious feeling of relief. She sank luxuriously into a chair. "I'm calling Charlie." Almost immediately she jumped up again and dashed to the phone. "This is too exciting to be real. I'm celebrating."

The other three had drifted into the living room and two minutes later, she joined them there. "Charlie's out, but his roommate said he'd give him the message." Too happy to contain her excitement, she added, "But I'm not sitting home alone. How about if I treat everyone to pizza tonight? The whole works on me."

"Sorry, Ellen." Derek looked up with a frown. "I've already made plans with Michelle."

"I'm getting together with a bunch of guys at the gym," Pat informed her, shifting the basketball from one hand to the other.

"And I told Mom I'd be home for dinner."

Some of the excitement drained from her, but she put on a brave front. "No problem. We'll do it another night."

"I'll go."

The small group whirled around, shocked to discover Reed standing there, framed in the living-room doorway.

CHAPTER FIVE

"REED," ELLEN BURST OUT, astonished. "When did you get here?" The instant she'd finished speaking, she realized how stupid the question was. He'd obviously just walked in the back door.

With a crooked grin, he checked his wristwatch. "About fifteen seconds ago."

"How was the trip?" Derek asked.

"Did you drive straight through?" Pat asked, then added, "I don't suppose you had a chance to see the Warriors play, did you?"

"You must be exhausted," Ellen said, noting how tired his eyes seemed.

As his smiling gaze met hers, the fine laugh lines that fanned out from his eyes became more pronounced. "I'm more hungry than tired. Didn't I just hear you offer to feed me pizza?"

"Ellen got a B-minus on her crazy algebra paper," Monte said with pride.

Rolling her eyes playfully toward the ceiling, Ellen laughed. "Who would have guessed it—I'm a mathematical genius!"

"So that's what this offer for dinner is all about. I thought you might have won the lottery."

He was more deeply tanned than Ellen remembered. Tanned. Vital. And incredibly male. He looked glad to be

home, she thought. Not a hint of hostility showed in the
eyes that smiled back at her.

"No such luck."

Derek made a show of glancing at his watch. "I'm out
of here or I'll be late picking up Michelle. It's good to see
you, Reed."

"Yeah, welcome home," Pat said, reaching for his
basketball. "I'll see you later."

Reed raised his right hand in salute and reached for his
suitcase, heading up the wide stairs. "Give me fifteen
minutes to shower and I'll meet you down here."

The minute Reed's back was turned, Monte placed his
hand over his heart and wildly batted his lashes as he
mouthed something about the beauty of love. Ellen
practically threw him out of the house, slamming the
door after him.

At the top of the stairs, Reed turned and glanced down
at her. "What was that all about?"

Ellen leaned against the closed door, her hand cover-
ing her mouth to smother her giggles. But the laughter
drained from her as she glanced at his puzzled face, and
she slowly straightened. She cleared her throat. "Nothing. Really. Did you want me to order the pizza and pick
it up? Or do you want to go out?"

"Whatever you prefer."

"If you leave it up to me, my choice would be to get
away from these four walls."

"I'll be ready in a few minutes."

Ellen suppressed a shudder at the thought of what
would have happened had Reed caught a glimpse of
Monte's antics. She herself handled the boys' teasing with
good-natured indulgence, but she was fairly sure that
Reed would take offense at their nonsense. And heaven

forbid that Danielle should ever catch a hint of what was going on—not that anything *was* going on.

With her thoughts becoming more muddled every minute, Ellen made her way to the third floor to change into a pair of gray tailored pants and a frilly pale-blue silk blouse. One glance in the mirror and she sadly shook her head. They were only going out for pizza—there was no need to wear anything so elaborate. Hurriedly, she changed into dark-brown cords and a turtleneck sweater the color of summer wheat. Then she ran a quick brush through her short curls and freshened her lipstick.

When Ellen returned to the living room, Reed was already waiting for her. "You're sure you don't mind going out?" she asked again.

"Are you dodging your pizza offer?"

He was so serious that Ellen couldn't help laughing. "Not in the least."

"Good. I hope you like spicy sausage with lots of olives."

"Love it."

His hand rested on her shoulder, warming her with his closeness. "And a cold beer."

"This is sounding better all the time." Ellen would have guessed Reed to be the type of man who drank martinis or expensive cocktails. In some ways, he was completely down-to-earth and in others, surprisingly complex. Perceptive, unpretentious and unpredictable; she knew that much about him, but she didn't expect to understand him soon.

Reed helped her into his pickup, which was parked in the driveway. The evening sky was already dark and Ellen regretted not having brought her coat.

"Cold?" Reed asked her when they stopped at a red light.

"Only a little."

He adjusted the switches for the heater and soon a rush of warm air filled the cab. Reed chatted easily, telling her a little about his project in California and explaining why his work demanded so much traveling. "That's changing now."

"Oh?" She couldn't restrain the little shiver of gladness that came with the announcement. "Will you be coming home more often?"

"Not for another three or four months. I'm up for promotion and then I'll be able to pick and choose my assignments more carefully. Over the past four years, I've traveled enough to last me a lifetime."

"Then it's true that there's no place like home."

"Be it ever so humble," he added with a chuckle.

"I don't exactly consider a three-story, twenty-room turn-of-the-century mansion all that humble."

"Add four college students and you'll quickly discover how unassuming it can become."

"Oh?"

"You like that word, don't you?"

"Yes," she agreed, her mouth curving into a lazy smile. "It's amazing how much you can say with that one little sound."

Reed exited from the freeway close to the Seattle Center and continued north. At her questioning glance he explained, "The best pizza in Seattle is made at a small place near the Center. You don't mind coming this far, do you?"

"Not at all. I'll travel a whole lot farther than this for a good pizza." Suddenly slouching forward, she pressed her forehead into her hand. "Oh, good grief, it's happening."

"What?"

"I'm beginning to sound like Monte."

They both laughed. It felt so good to be sitting there with Reed, sharing an easy, relaxed companionship, that Ellen could almost forget about Danielle. Almost, but not quite.

Although Ellen had said she'd pay for the pizza, Reed insisted on picking up the tab. They sat across from each other at a narrow booth in the corner of the semidarkened room. A lighted red candle in a glass bowl flickered on the table between them and Ellen decided this was the sum total of atmosphere. The inevitable jukebox blared out the latest country hits, drowning out the possibility of any audible conversation, which seemed just as well since she was beginning to feel strangely tongue-tied.

When their number was called, Reed slid from the booth and returned a minute later with two frothy beer in ice-cold mugs and a huge steaming pizza.

"I hope you don't expect us to eat all this?" Ellen asked anxiously, shouting above the music. The pizza certainly smelled enticing, but Ellen doubted that she'd manage to eat more than two or three pieces.

"We'll put a decent dent in it, anyway," Reed said, resuming his seat. "I bought their largest, thinking the boys would appreciate any leftovers as a midnight snack."

"You're a terrific older brother."

The fast-paced rhythms of the song on the jukebox were fading into silence at last.

"There are times when I'd like to shake some sense into Derek, though," Reed said without elaborating.

Ellen dropped her gaze to the spicy pizza and lifted a small slice onto her plate. Strings of melted cheese still linked the piece to the rest of the pie. She pulled them loose and licked her fingers. "I can imagine how you felt when you discovered that Derek had accidentally-on-purpose forgotten to tell you about renting out bedrooms.''

Reed shrugged noncommittally. ''I was thinking more about the time he let you climb on top of the roof,'' he muttered.

''He didn't *let* me, I went, all by myself.''

''But you won't do it again. Right?''

''Right,'' Ellen agreed reluctantly. Behind Reed's slow smiles and easy banter, she recognized a solid wall of unrelenting male pride. ''You still haven't forgiven me for that, have you?''

''Not you. Derek.''

''I think this is one of those subjects where we should agree to disagree.'' It astonished Ellen that within the space of a few words they could find something to argue about.

''Have you heard from your mother?'' Reed asked, apparently just as willing to change the subject and avoid an argument. Ellen nodded. ''She seems very happy and after a day or two, I discovered I couldn't be more pleased for her. She's worked hard all these years and deserves a lot of contentment.''

''I knew you'd soon realize that.'' Warmth briefly showed in his green eyes.

''I felt a whole lot better just talking to you. It was a surprise when Mom announced her marriage, but it shouldn't have been. The signs were there all along. I suppose once the three of us kids were gone, she felt free to remarry. And I suppose she thought that presenting it to the family as an accomplished fact would make it easier for all of us.''

There was a comfortable silence between them as they finished eating. The pizza was thick with sausage and cheese and Ellen placed her hands on her stomach after leisurely munching two narrow pieces. "I'm stuffed," she declared, leaning back. "But you're right, this has got to be the best pizza in town."

"I thought you'd like it."

Reed brought over a carry-out box and Ellen carefully put the leftovers inside.

"How about a movie?" he asked once they were in the parking lot.

Astounded, Ellen darted him a sideways glance, but his features were shadowed and unreadable. "You're kidding, aren't you?"

"I wouldn't have asked you if I was."

"But you must be exhausted." Ellen guessed that he'd probably spent most of the day driving.

"A little," he admitted.

Her frown deepened. Suddenly, it no longer seemed right for them to be together. The problem was that Ellen had been so pleased to see him that she hadn't stopped to think about the consequences of their going out together. "Thanks anyway, but it's been a long week. I think I'll call it an early night."

When they reached the house, Reed parked on the street, rather than the driveway. The light from the stars and the silvery moon penetrated the tree limbs that hung overhead and created shadows on his face. Neither of them seemed eager to leave the warm cab of the pickup truck. The mood was intimate and Ellen didn't want to disturb this moment of tranquility. Lowering her gaze, she admitted to herself how attracted she was to Reed and how much she liked him. She admitted, too, that it was wrong for her to feel this way about him.

"You're quiet all of a sudden."

Ellen's smile was decidedly forced. She turned toward him to apologize for putting a damper on their evening, but the words never left her lips. Instead her eyes met his in a slow, sensual exchange. Paralyzed, Ellen stared at Reed, battling to disguise the intense attraction she felt for him. It seemed the most natural thing in the world to lean toward him and brush her lips over his. She could smell the woodsy scent of his after-shave and could almost taste his mouth over hers. With the determined force of her will, she pulled her gaze away and reached for the door, like a drowning person grasping a life preserver.

She was on the front porch by the time Reed joined her. Her fingers shook as she inserted the key into the lock.

"Ellen." He spoke her name softly and placed his hand on her shoulder.

"I don't know why we went out tonight." Her voice was high and strained as she drew free of his touch. "We had no business being together."

In response, Reed mockingly lifted one eyebrow. "I believe it was you who asked me."

"Be serious, will you," she snapped irritably and shoved open the door.

Reed slammed it shut behind him and followed her into the kitchen. He set the pizza on the counter and turned to face her. "What the hell do you mean? I *was* being serious."

"You shouldn't have been with me tonight."

"Why not?"

"Where's Danielle? I'm not the one who's been patiently waiting around for you. She is. You had no business taking me out to dinner and then suggesting a movie. You're my landlord, not my boyfriend."

"Let's get two things straight here. First, what's between Danielle and me is none of your business. And second, you invited *me* out. Remember?"

"But...it wasn't like that and you know it."

"Besides, I thought you claimed you were far too old for 'boyfriends.'" She detected an undertone of amusement in his low-pitched voice.

Confused, Ellen marched into the living room and immediately busied herself straightening magazines. Reed charged in after her, leaving the kitchen door swinging in his wake. Defensively clutching a sofa pillow to her stomach, Ellen searched for some witty retort. Naturally, when she needed a clever comeback, her mind was a total blank.

"You're making a joke out of everything," she told him, damning her voice for shaking. "And I don't appreciate that. If you want to play games, do it with someone other than me."

"Ellen, listen—"

The phone rang and she jerked her attention to the hallway.

"I didn't mean—" Reed paused and raked his fingers through his hair. The phone pealed a second time. "Go ahead and answer that."

She hurried away, relieved to interrupt this disturbing conversation. "Hello." Her voice sounded breathless, as though she'd raced down the stairs.

"Ellen? This is Charlie. I got a message that you phoned."

For one crazy instant, Ellen forgot why she'd wanted to talk to Charlie. "I phoned? Oh, right. Remember that algebra paper I was struggling with? Well, it came back today."

"How'd you do?"

A little of the surprised pleasure returned. "I still can't believe it. I got a B-minus. My simple paper about the wonders of the number nine received one of the highest marks in the class. I'm still in shock."

The sound of Charlie's delighted chuckle came over the wire. "This calls for a celebration. How about if we go out tomorrow night? Dinner, drinks, the works."

Ellen almost regretted the impulse to contact Charlie. She sincerely liked him, and she hated the thought of stringing him along or taking advantage of his attraction to her. "Nothing so elaborate. Chinese food and a movie would be great."

"You let me worry about that. Just be ready by seven."

"Charlie, listen—"

"No arguing. I'll see you at seven."

By the time Ellen was off the phone, Reed was nowhere to be seen. Nor was he around the following afternoon. The boys didn't comment and she couldn't very well ask about him without arousing their suspicions. As it was, the less she mentioned Reed around those three, the better. The boys had obviously read more into the letter, phone call and dinner than Reed had intended. But she couldn't blame them; she'd read enough into it herself to be frightened by what was happening between them. He'd almost kissed her when he'd parked in front of the house. And she'd wanted him to—that was what disturbed her most. But if she allowed her emotions to get involved, she knew that someone would probably end up being hurt. And the most likely "someone" was Ellen herself.

Besides, if Reed was attracted to Danielle's sleek elegance, then he would hardly be interested in her own more homespun qualities.

A few minutes before seven, Ellen was ready for her evening with Charlie. She stood before the downstairs hallway mirror to put the finishing touches to her appearance, fastening her gold earrings and straightening the single chain necklace that graced her slender neck.

"Where's Reed been today?" Pat inquired of no one in particular.

"His sports car is gone," Monte offered, munching on a chocolate bar. "I noticed it wasn't in the garage when I took out the garbage."

Slowly Ellen sauntered into the living room. She didn't want to appear too curious, but at the same time, she was definitely interested in listening to the conversation.

She had flopped into a chair and picked up a two-month-old magazine before she noticed all three boys staring at her.

"What are you looking at me for?"

"We thought you might know something."

"About what?" she asked, playing dumb.

"Reed," all three said simultaneously.

"Why should I know anything?" Her gaze flittered from them to the magazine and back again.

"You went out with him last night."

"We didn't *go out* the way you're implying."

Pat, with the basketball still tucked under one arm, pointed an accusing finger at her. "The two of you were alone together and both of you have been acting weird ever since."

"And I say all three of you have overactive imaginations."

"All I know is that Reed was like a wounded bear this morning," Derek volunteered.

"Everyone's entitled to an off day." Hoping to give a casual impression, she leafed through the magazine, idly fanning the pages with her thumb.

"That might explain Reed. But what about you?"

"Me?"

"For the first time since you moved in, you weren't downstairs until after ten."

"I slept in. Is that a crime?"

"It just might be. You and Reed are both behaving real strange. It's like the two of you are avoiding each other and we want to know why."

"It's your imagination. Believe me, if there was anything to tell you, I would."

"Sure, you would," Derek mocked.

From the corner of her eye, Ellen noticed Charlie's car pull up in front of the house. Releasing a sigh of relief, she quickly stood and gave the boys a falsely bright smile. "If you'll excuse me, my date has arrived."

"Should we tell Reed you're out with Charlie if he wants to know where you are?" Monte looked uncomfortable asking the question.

"Of course. Besides, he probably already knows. He's free to see anyone he wants and so am I. For that matter, so are you." Walking backward as she spoke, she made her way toward the front door and pulled it open before Charlie even got a chance to ring the doorbell.

The evening didn't go well. Charlie took her out for a steak dinner and spent more money than Ellen knew he could afford. More and more, she regretted having phoned him. Charlie had obviously interpreted her call as a sign that she was interested in becoming romantically involved. She wasn't, and didn't know how to make it clear without offending him.

"Did you have a good time?" he asked as they drove back toward Capitol Hill.

"Lovely, thank you, Charlie."

His hand reached for hers and squeezed it reassuringly. "We don't go out enough."

"Neither of us can afford it too often."

"We don't need to go to a fancy restaurant to be together," he contradicted lightly. "Just being with you is a joy."

"Thank you." If only Charlie weren't so nice. She hated the idea of hurting him. But she couldn't allow him to go on hoping that she might ever return his feelings. As much as she dreaded it, she knew she had to disillusion him. Anything else would be cruel and dishonest.

"I don't think I've made a secret of how I feel about you, Ellen. You're wonderful."

"Come on, Charlie, I'm not that different from a thousand other girls on campus." She tried to swallow the tightness in her throat. "In fact, I was noticing the way that girl in our third-period class—what's her name—Lisa, has been looking at you lately."

"I hadn't noticed."

"I believe you've got yourself an admirer."

"But I'm only interested in you."

"Charlie, listen, please. I think you're a wonderful person. I—"

"Shh," he demanded softly as he parked in front of Ellen's house and turned off the engine. He slid his arm along the back of the seat and caressed her shoulder. "I don't want you to say anything."

"But I feel that I may have—"

"Ellen," he whispered her name seductively. "Be quiet and just let me kiss you."

Before she could utter another word, Charlie claimed her mouth in a short but surprisingly ardent kiss. Charlie had kissed her on several occasions, but never had she allowed their lovemaking to go beyond the most innocent of exchanges.

When his arms tightened around her, Ellen resisted.

"Invite me in for coffee," he whispered urgently in her ear.

She pressed her forehead against his shirt collar. "Not tonight."

He tensed. "Can I see you again soon?"

"I don't know. We see each other every day. Why don't we just meet after class for a coffee one day next week?"

"But I want so much more than that," he protested.

"I know," she answered, dropping her eyes. She felt confused and miserable.

Ellen could tell he was disappointed just by the way he climbed out of the car and trudged around to her side. There was tense silence between them as he walked her up to the front door and kissed her a second time. Again, Ellen had to break away from him by pushing her hands against his chest.

"Thank you for everything," she whispered.

"Right. Thanks, but no thanks."

"Oh, Charlie, don't start that. Not now."

Eyes downcast, he wearily rubbed a hand along the side of his face. "I guess I'll see you Monday," he said with a sigh.

"Thanks for the lovely evening." She didn't let herself inside until Charlie had climbed into his car and driven away.

Releasing a jagged breath, Ellen had just started to unbutton her coat when she glanced up to find Reed standing in the living room, glowering at her.

"Is something wrong?" The undisguised anger that twisted his mouth and hardened his gaze was a shock.

"Do you always linger outside with your boy-friends?"

"We didn't linger."

"Right." He dragged one hand roughly through his hair and marched a few paces toward her, only to do an abrupt about-face. "I saw the two of you necking."

"Necking?" Ellen was so startled by his unreasonable anger that she didn't know whether to laugh or argue. "Be serious, will you? Two chaste kisses hardly constitute necking."

"What kind of influence are you on Derek and the others?" He couldn't seem to stand still and paced back and forth in agitation.

He was obviously furious, but Ellen was at a loss to understand the real reason for his anger. He couldn't possibly believe those absurd insinuations. Perhaps he was upset about something else and merely taking it out on her, she reasoned. "Reed, what's wrong?" she finally asked.

"I saw you out there."

"You were spying on me?"

"I wasn't spying," he snapped.

"Charlie and I were inside his car. You must have been staring out the windows to have even seen us."

He didn't answer her, but instead hurled another accusation in her direction. "You're corrupting the boys."

"I'm what?" She couldn't believe what she was hearing. "They're nineteen years old. Trust me, they've kissed girls before now."

"You can kiss anyone you like. Just don't do it in front of the boys."

From the way this conversation was going, Ellen could see that Reed was in no mood to listen to reason. "I think it would be better if we discussed this issue another time," she said quietly.

"We'll talk about it right now."

Ignoring his domineering tone as much as possible, Ellen forced a smile. "Good night, Reed. I'll see you in the morning."

She was halfway to the stairs when he called her, his voice calm. "Ellen."

She turned around, holding herself tense, watching him stride quickly across the short distance that separated them. His thumb and forefinger captured her chin, tilting it slightly so he could study her face. Gently, he rubbed his thumb across her lips. "Funny, you don't look kissed."

In one breath he was accusing her of necking and in the next, claiming she was unkissed. Not knowing how to respond, Ellen didn't. She merely gazed at him, her eyes wide and questioning.

"If you're going to engage in that sort of activity, the least you can do—" He paused. With each word his mouth drew closer and closer to hers until his lips hovered over her own and their breaths mingled. "The least you can do is look kissed." His hand located the vein pounding wildly in her throat as his mouth settled over hers. The kiss leisurely explored her lips as he worked his way from one side of her mouth to the other. She felt the full weight of his muscular body against her own, and its heat seemed to melt her very bones.

Slowly, patiently, his mouth moved over hers with a petal softness, an exquisite tenderness that left her quivering with anticipation and delight. Timidly, her hands crept across his chest to link behind his neck. Again his lips descended on hers, more hungrily now, as he groaned and pulled her even closer.

Ellen felt her face grow hot as she surrendered to the heavenly sensations that stole through her like the gentle fog of an early spring. Yet all the while, her mind was telling her she had no right to feel this contentment, this warmth. Reed belonged to another woman. Not to her . . . to someone else.

Her breath caught as he twisted his mouth away from hers. His labored breathing was audible. "I was afraid of that," he mumbled.

"Of what?" she asked uncertainly.

"You taste too good. Like cotton candy," he moaned.

Color seeped into her face. When she'd realized that he intended to kiss her, her first thought had been to resist. But once she'd felt his mouth on hers, all her resolve had drained away. Embarrassed now, she realized that she'd pliantly wrapped her arms around his neck. And worse, she'd responded with enough enthusiasm for him to know exactly what she was feeling.

He pressed his mouth to the corner of her forehead as though he couldn't bear to release her.

Ellen struggled to breathe normally. She let her arms slip from his neck to his chest and through the palm of her hand, she could feel the rapid beating of his heart. She closed her eyes, knowing that her own pulse was pounding no less wildly.

She could feel his mouth move against her temple. "I've been wanting to do that for days." The grudging admission came low and taut.

The words to tell him that she'd wanted it just as much were quickly silenced by the sound of someone walking into the room.

Guiltily Reed and Ellen jerked apart. Her face turned a deep shade of red as Derek stopped in his tracks, staring at them.

"Hi."

"Hi." Reed and Ellen said together.

"Hey, I'm not interrupting anything, am I? If you like, I could turn around and pretend I didn't see a thing."

"Do it," Reed ordered.

"No," Ellen said just as quickly.

Derek's eyes sparkled with boyish delight. "You know," he said, "I had a feeling about the two of you from the beginning." While he spoke, he was taking small steps backward, until he stood pressed against the polished kitchen door. "Right on." He gave his brother the thumbs-up sign as he nudged open the door with one foot and hurriedly backed out of the room.

"Now look what you've done," Ellen wailed.

"Me? As I recall you were just as eager for this as I was."

"It was a mistake," she blurted out. A ridiculous, illogical mistake. He had accused her of being a bad influence on the boys and then proceeded to kiss her senseless.

"You're telling me." A distinct coolness entered his eyes. "It's probably a damn good thing I'm leaving."

There was no hiding the stricken look. "Again? So soon?"

"After what's just happened, I'd say it wasn't nearly soon enough."

"But . . . where to this time?"

"Denver. But I'll be back before Thanksgiving."

Mentally, Ellen calculated that he'd be away another two weeks.

When he spoke again, his voice was gentle. "It's just as well, don't you think?"

CHAPTER SIX

"IT LOOKS LIKE RAIN." Pat stood in front of the window above the kitchen sink and frowned at the thick black clouds that darkened the late afternoon sky. "Why does it have to rain?"

Ellen turned over her sister's letter and glanced up at him. "Are you seeking a scientific response or will a simple 'I don't know' suffice?"

The kitchen door swung open and Derek sauntered in. "Has anyone seen Reed?"

Instantly, Ellen's gaze dropped to her sister's letter. Reed had returned to Seattle two days earlier and so far, they'd done an admirable job of avoiding each other. Both mornings, he'd left for his office before she was up. Each evening, he'd come home, showered, changed clothes and then gone off again. It didn't require much detective work to figure out that he was with Danielle. Ellen had attempted—unsuccessfully—not to think of Reed at all. And especially not of him and Danielle together.

For her part, she secretly wished that she'd had the nerve to arrange an opportunity to talk to Reed. So much remained unclear in her mind. Reed had kissed her and it had been wonderful, yet that was something neither seemed willing to admit. It was as if they had tacitly agreed that the kiss had been a terrible mistake and should be forgotten. The problem was, Ellen couldn't force the memory of his touch from her troubled mind.

"Reed hasn't been around the house much," Pat answered.

"I know." Derek sounded slightly disgruntled and cast an accusing glance in Ellen's direction. "It's almost like he doesn't live here anymore."

"He doesn't. Not really." Pat stepped away from the window and gently set the basketball on a chair. "It's sort of like he's a guest who stops in now and then."

Ellen preferred not to be drawn into this conversation. She hastily folded her letter, slid it back inside the envelope and stood up to leave.

"Say, Ellen." Pat stopped her.

She muttered something disparaging under her breath about almost making a clean getaway. Turning, she met his questioning gaze with a nervous smile. "Yes?"

"I'll be leaving in a few minutes. Have a nice Thanksgiving."

Relieved that the subject of Reed had been dropped, she threw him a brilliant smile. "You, too."

"Where are you having dinner tomorrow?" Derek asked, as if the thought had unexpectedly occurred to him.

Her mother was still in Arizona, her sister had gone to visit her in-laws and Bud couldn't get leave, so Ellen had decided to stay in Seattle. "Here."

"In this house?" Derek's eyes widened with concern. "But why? Shouldn't you be with your family?"

"My family is going in different directions this year. It's no problem. In fact, I'm looking forward to having the whole house to myself."

"There isn't any reason to spend the day alone," Derek argued. "My parents wouldn't mind putting out an extra plate. There's always plenty of food."

Her heart was touched by the sincerity of his invitation. "Thank you, but honestly, I prefer it this way."

"It's because of Reed, isn't it?" Both boys studied her with wide, inquisitive eyes.

"Nonsense."

"But, Ellen, he isn't going to be there."

"Reed isn't the reason," she assured him. Undoubtedly, Reed would be spending the holiday with Danielle. She made an effort to ignore the instant flash of pain that accompanied the thought; she knew she had no right to feel hurt if Reed chose to spend Thanksgiving with his "almost" fiancée. The other woman had a prior claim.

"You're sure?" Derek didn't look convinced.

"You could come and spend the day with my family," Pat offered next.

"Will you two quit acting like it's such a terrible tragedy? I'm going to *enjoy* an entire day alone. Look at these nails." She fanned her fingers and held them up for their inspection. "For once, I'll have an uninterrupted block of time to do all the things I've delayed for weeks."

"All right, but if you change your mind, give me a call."

"I asked her first," Derek argued. "You'll call me. Right?"

"Right to you both."

THANKSGIVING MORNING, Ellen woke to a torrential downpour. Thick drops of rain pelted against the window and the day seemed destined to be a melancholy one. Lazily, she lounged in her room and read, enjoying the

luxury of not having to rush around, preparing breakfast for the whole household.

She wandered down to the kitchen, where she was
greeted by a heavy silence. The house was definitely
empty. Apparently, Reed, too, had started his day early.
Ellen couldn't decide whether she was pleased or an-
noyed that she had seen so little of him since his return
from Denver. He'd been the one to avoid her, and she'd
concluded that two could play his silly game. So she'd
purposely stayed out of his way. A sad smile touched her
eyes as she reflected on the past few days. She and Reed
had been acting like a pair of adolescents.

She ate a bowl of cornflakes and spent the next hour
wiping down the cupboards, with the radio tuned to the
soft-rock music station. Whenever a particularly romantic ballad aired, she danced around the kitchen with
an imaginary partner. Not so imaginary, really. In her
mind, she was in Reed's arms.

The silence became more oppressive during the afternoon, while Ellen busied herself fussing over her nails.
When the final application of polish had dried, she decided to flip on the television to drown out the quiet. An
hour into the football game, Ellen noticed that it was
nearly dinnertime, and she suddenly felt hungry.

Popcorn sounded wonderful, so she popped a small
batch and splurged by dripping melted butter over the
top. She carried the bowl into the living room and
climbed back onto the sofa, tucking her legs under her.
She had just found a comfortable position when she
heard a noise in the kitchen.

Frowning, she twisted around, wondering who it could
possibly be.

The door into the living room swung open and Ellen's
heart rate soared into double time.

"Reed?" She blinked to make sure he wasn't an apparition.

"Hello."

He didn't vanish. Instead he took several steps in her direction. "That popcorn smells great."

Without considering the wisdom of her offer, she held out the bowl to him. "Help yourself."

"Thanks." He took off his suit coat and tossed it over the back of a chair before joining her on the sofa. He leaned forward, studying the television screen. "Who's winning?"

Ellen was momentarily confused, until she realized he was asking about the football game. "I don't know. I haven't paid that much attention."

Reed reached for another handful of popcorn and Ellen set the bowl in the center of the coffee table. Her emotions were muddled. She couldn't imagine what Reed was doing at the house with her. He was supposed to be at Danielle's. Although the question burned in her mind, she couldn't bring herself to ask it. She glanced at him covertly through her lashes, but Reed was staring at the television as though he were alone in the room.

"I'll get us something to drink," she volunteered.

"Great."

Even while she was speaking, Reed hadn't looked in her direction. Slightly piqued by his attitude, she stalked into the kitchen and took two Pepsis out of the refrigerator.

When she returned with the soft drinks and two glasses filled with ice, Reed reached out and took one set from her. "Thanks," he murmured, popping open the can. He carefully poured the soda over the ice and set the can aside before taking a sip.

"You're welcome," she grumbled and flopped down again, pretending to watch television. But her mind was spinning in a hundred different directions. When she couldn't tolerate it any longer, she blurted out the question that dominated her thoughts, her voice high and agitated.

"Reed, what are you doing here?"

He took a long swallow before answering her. "I happen to live here."

"You know what I mean. You should be with Danielle."

"I was, earlier, but I decided I preferred your company."

"I don't need your sympathy," she snapped, then swallowed painfully and averted her gaze. Her fingers tightened around the cold glass until the chill extended up her arm. "I'm perfectly content to spend the day alone. I just wish everyone would kindly refrain from saving me from myself."

His low chuckle was unexpected. "That wasn't my intention."

"Then why are you here?"

"I already told you."

"I don't accept that," she said shakily. He was toying with her emotions, and the thought made her all the more furious.

"All right." Determinedly, he set down his drink and turned toward her. "I thought this was the perfect opportunity for us to talk."

Her eyes were clouded with anger as she met his steady gaze. "You haven't said more than ten words to me in three days. What makes this one day so special?"

"We're alone, aren't we, and that's more than we can usually say." His voice was strained. He hesitated a moment, his lips pressed together in a thin, hard line. "I don't know what's happening with us."

"Nothing's happening," she said wildly. "You kissed me, and we both admitted it was a terrible mistake. Can't we leave it at that?"

"No," he answered dryly. "I don't believe it was such a major tragedy, and neither do you."

If it really had been a mistake, Ellen wouldn't have remembered it with such vivid clarity. Nor would she yearn for the taste of him again and again, or hurt so much when she knew he was with Danielle.

Swiftly she turned her eyes away from the disturbing intensity of his, unwilling to reveal the depth of her feelings.

"It wasn't a mistake, was it, Ellen?" he prompted in a husky voice.

She squeezed her eyes shut and shook her head. "No," she whispered, but the word was barely audible.

His arms gathered her close to the warmth of his taut, muscular chest. She felt his deep shudder of satisfaction as he buried his face in her hair. Long moments passed before he spoke. "Nothing that felt so right could have been a mistake."

Tenderly he kissed her, his lips touching hers with a gentleness she hadn't expected. As if he feared she was somehow fragile; as if he found her highly precious. Without conscious decision, her arms slipped around him as she opened her mouth to his, savoring this moment.

"The whole time Danielle and I were together this afternoon, I was wishing it was you. Today, of all days, it seemed important to be with you."

Ellen gazed up into his eyes and saw not only his gentleness, but his confusion. Her fingers slid into the thick hair around his lean, rugged face. "I don't imagine Danielle was pleased to have you leave."

"She wasn't. I didn't even know how to explain it to her. Hell, I don't know how to explain it to myself."

Ellen swallowed down the dryness that constricted her throat. "Do you want me to move out of the house?"

"No," he said forcefully, then added more quietly, "I think I'd go crazy if you did. Are you a witch who's cast some spell over me?"

She tried unsuccessfully to answer him, but no words of denial came. The knowledge that he was experiencing these strange whirling emotions was enough to overwhelm her.

"If so, the spell is working," he murmured, although he didn't sound particularly pleased at the idea.

"I'm confused, too," she admitted and pressed her forehead to his chest. She could feel his heart pounding beneath her open hand.

His long fingers stroked her hair. "I know." Gently he leaned down and kissed the top of her head. "The night you went out with Charlie, I was completely unreasonable. I need to apologize for the things I said to you. To put it plain and simple, I was jealous. I've admitted that, these last weeks in Denver." Some of the tightness left his voice, as though the events of that night had weighed heavily on his mind. "I didn't like the idea of another man holding you and when I saw the two of you kissing, I think I went a little berserk."

"I . . . we don't date often."

"I won't ask you not to see him again," he said reluctantly. "I can't ask anything of you."

"Nor can I ask anything of you."

His grip around her tightened. "Let's give this time."

"It's the only thing we can do."

Reed straightened and draped his arm around Ellen's shoulders, drawing her protectively close to his side. Her head nestled neatly against his chest. "I'd like for us to start going out together," he said, his chin resting on the crown of her head. "Will that cause a problem for you?"

"Cause a problem?" she repeated uncertainly.

"I'm thinking about the boys."

Remembering their earlier buffoonery and the way they'd taken such delight in teasing her, Ellen shook her head. If those three had any evidence at all of a romance between Reed and her, they could make everyone's lives miserable. "I don't know."

"Then let's play it cool for a while. We'll work into this gradually until they become accustomed to seeing us together and it won't be any big deal."

"I think you might be right." She didn't like pretense or deceit, but she'd be the one subjected to their good-natured heckling. They wouldn't dare try it with Reed.

"Can I take you to dinner tomorrow night?"

"I'd like that."

"Not as much as I will. But how are we going to do this? It'll be obvious that we're going out together," he mused aloud.

"Not if we leave the house at different times," she countered.

She could feel his frown. "Is that really necessary?"

A sigh worked its way through her. "I'm afraid so."

Ellen and Reed spent the remainder of the evening doing nothing more exciting than watching television. His arm remained securely around her shoulders and she felt a sense of deep contentment that was new to her. It was a peaceful interlude in a time that had become increasingly wrought with stress.

Derek arrived back at the house close to nine-thirty. They both heard him lope in through the kitchen and Reed gave Ellen a quick kiss before withdrawing his arm.

"Hi." Derek entered the room and stood beside the sofa, shuffling his feet. "Dad wondered where you were." His gaze flitted from Ellen back to his brother.

"I told them I wouldn't be there for dinner."

"I know. But Danielle phoned looking for you."

"She knew where I was."

"Apparently not." Reed's younger brother tucked one hand in the side pocket of his dress pants. "Are you two friends again?"

Reed's eyes found Ellen's and he smiled warmly. "You could say that."

"Good. Neither of you have been the easiest people to be around lately." Without giving them a chance to reply, he whirled around and marched upstairs.

Ellen placed a hand over her mouth to smother her giggles. "Well, he certainly told us."

Amusement flared in Reed's eyes, and he chuckled softly. "I guess he did, at that." His arm slid around Ellen's shoulders once again. "Have you been bitchy lately, my dear?"

"I'm never bitchy," she returned.

"Me neither."

They exchanged smiles and went back to watching their movie.

As much as Ellen tried to concentrate on the television, her mind unwillingly returned to Derek's announcement. "Do you think you should call Danielle?" Her lashes fluttered downward, disguising her discomfort. Having Reed with her these past few hours had been like an unexpected Christmas gift, granted early. But she felt guilty that it had been at the other woman's expense.

Impatience tightened Reed's mouth. "Maybe I'd better. I didn't mean to offend her or her family by leaving early." He seemed to measure his words as he spoke. He paused a moment, then added, "Danielle is a little high-strung."

Ellen had certainly noticed, but she had no intention of mentioning it. And she had no intention of listening in on their conversation. "While you're doing that, I think I'll wash up the popcorn dishes and call it a night."

Reed's eyes widened slightly in a mock reprimand. "It's a little early, isn't it?"

"Perhaps," she said, faking a yawn, "but I've got this hot date tomorrow night and I want to be well rested for it."

The front door opened and Pat sauntered in. "Hi." He stopped and studied them curiously. "Hi," he repeated.

"I thought you were staying home for the weekend." Ellen remembered that Pat had said something about being gone for the entire four-day holiday.

"Mom gave my bedroom to one of my aunts. I can't see any reason to sleep on the floor when I've got a bed here."

"That makes sense," Reed said dryly.

"Are you two getting along again?"

"We never fought."

"Yeah, sure," Pat mumbled sarcastically. "And a basket isn't worth two points."

Ellen had been unaware how much her disagreement with Reed had affected the boys. Apparently, Reed's reaction was the same as hers; their eyes met briefly in silent communication.

"I'll go up with you," she told Pat. "See you in the morning, Reed."

"Right."

Halfway up the stairs, Pat tossed her the basketball. "Here, catch."

She caught it nimbly and flung it back. "One of these days you're going to discover something more exciting than sports."

"Yeah?"

"Yeah." She laughed and left him on the second floor to trudge her way up to the third.

It shouldn't have been a surprise that she slept so well. Her mind was at ease and she awoke feeling contented and hopeful. Neither of them were making any commitments yet. They didn't know if what they felt would last a day or a lifetime. They were explorers, discovering the uncharted territory of a new relationship. Ellen felt wonderful.

Humming, she bounded down the stairs early the next morning. Reed was already up, sitting at the kitchen table drinking coffee and reading the paper.

"Morning," she offered, pouring water into the tea kettle and setting it on the burner.

"Morning." His eyes didn't leave the paper.

Ellen brought down a mug from the cupboard and walked past Reed on her way to get the canister of tea. His hand reached out and gripped her around the waist, pulling her down into his lap.

Before she could protest, his mouth firmly covered hers. When the kiss was over, Ellen straightened, resting her hands on his shoulders. "What was that for?" she asked to disguise how flustered he made her feel.

"Just to say good morning," he said in a warm, husky voice. "I don't imagine I'll have too many opportunities to do it in such a pleasant manner."

"No," she said and cleared her throat. "Probably not."

Ellen was sitting at the table, with a section of the paper propped up in front of her, when the boys came into the kitchen.

"Morning," Monte murmured vaguely as he opened the refrigerator. He was barefoot, his hair was uncombed and his shirt was still unbuttoned. "What's for breakfast?"

"Whatever your little heart desires," she told him, neatly folding over a page of the newspaper.

"Does this mean you're not cooking?"

"That's right."

"But—"

Reed lowered the sports page and glared openly at Monte.

"Cold cereal will be fine," Monte grumbled and took down a large serving bowl, emptying half the contents of a box of rice crisps inside.

"Hey, save some for me," Pat hollered from the doorway. "That's my favorite."

"I was here first."

Derek strolled into the kitchen. "Does everyone have to argue?"

"Everyone?" Reed cocked a mocking brow in his brother's direction.

"First it was you and Ellen, and now it's Pat and Monte."

"Hey, that's right," Monte cried. "You two aren't fighting. That's great." He set his serving bowl of rice crisps on the table. "Does this mean...you're...you know."

Lowering the paper, Ellen eyed him sardonically. "No, I don't know."

"You know...seeing each other?" A deep flush darkened Monte's face.

"We see each other every day."

"That's not what I mean."

"But that's all I'm answering." From the corner of her eye, she caught sight of Pat pantomiming a fiddler, and she groaned inwardly. The boys were going to make it difficult to maintain any kind of romantic relationship with Reed. She cast him a speculative glance. But if Reed had noticed the activity around him, he wasn't letting on, and Ellen was grateful.

"I've got a practice game tonight," Pat told Ellen as he buttered a piece of toast. "Do you want to come?"

Flustered, her gaze automatically sought out Reed. "Sorry... I'd like to come, but I've got a date."

"Bring him along."

"I... don't know if he appreciates basketball."

"Yeah, he does," Derek supplied. "Charlie and I were talking about it recently and he said it's one of his favorite games."

She didn't want to tell an outright lie. But she would save herself a lot of aggravation if she simply let Derek and the others assume it was Charlie she'd be seeing.

"What about you, Reed?"

His gaze didn't flicker from the paper and Ellen marveled at his ability to appear so dispassionate. "Not tonight. Thanks anyway."

"Have you got a date, as well?" Derek pressed.

It seemed as though everyone in the kitchen was watching Reed, waiting for his response. "I generally go out Friday nights."

"Well," Ellen said, coming to her feet. "I think I'll get moving. I want to take advantage of the holiday to do some errands. Does anybody need anything picked up at the cleaners?"

"I do," Monte said, raising his hand. "If you'll wait a minute, I'll get the slip."

"Sure."

By some miracle, Ellen was able to avoid any more questions for the remainder of the day. She busily went about her errands and didn't see Reed until late in the afternoon, when their paths happened to cross in the kitchen. He quickly whispered the time and meeting place and explained that he'd leave first. Ellen didn't have a chance to do more than agree before the boys were upon them, their eyes wide and questioning.

At precisely seven, Ellen met Reed at the grocery parking lot two blocks from the house. He'd left ten minutes earlier to wait for her there. As soon as he spotted her, he leaned across the cab of the pickup and opened the door on her side. Ellen found it slightly amusing that when he was with her, he drove the pickup, and when he was with Danielle he took the sports car. She wondered whether or not this was a conscious decision. In any event, it told her quite a bit about the way Reed viewed the two women in his life.

"Did you get away unscathed?" he asked, chuckling softly.

She slid into the seat beside him in the cab and shook her head. "Not entirely. All three were curious about why Charlie wasn't coming to the house to pick me up. I didn't want to lie, so I told them they'd have to ask him."

"Will they?"

"I certainly hope not."

Reed's hand reached for hers and his eyes grew serious. "I'm not convinced that keeping this a secret is the right thing to do."

"I don't like it either, but it's better than being the constant brunt of their teasing."

"I'll put a stop to that." His voice dropped ominously and Ellen didn't doubt that he'd quickly handle the situation.

"But, Reed, they're just having a little innocent fun. They don't mean any harm. I was hoping we could lead them gradually into accepting us as a couple. Let them get used to seeing us together before we spring it on them that we're...dating." She used that term for lack of a better one.

"Ellen, I don't know."

"Trust me on this," she pleaded, her round eyes imploring him. This arrangement, with its secrecy and deception, was far from ideal, but for now, she thought, it was necessary.

His kiss was brief and ardent. "I don't think I could deny you anything." But he didn't sound happy about it.

The restaurant to which Reed took her was located in the south end of Seattle, thirty minutes from Capitol Hill. Ellen was mildly surprised that he chose one so far from home but didn't mention it. The food was fantastic and the view from the Des Moines Marina alone would have been worth the drive.

Reed ordered a bottle of an award-winning Chardonnay that came from a local winery. It was satisfyingly clear and crisp.

"I spoke to Danielle," Reed began.

"Reed." She stopped him, placing her hand over his. "What goes on between you and Danielle has nothing to do with me. We've made no promises and no commitments." In fact, of course, she was dying to know about the other woman Reed had dated for so long. She hoped that if she pretended no interest in his relationship with Danielle, she'd seem much smoother and more sophisticated then she really was.

He looked a little stunned. "But—"

Swiftly she lowered her gaze. "I don't want to know." Naturally, she was longing to hear every sordid detail. As it was, she felt incredibly guilty about the other woman. Danielle might have had her faults, but she loved Reed. She must have, to be so patient with his traveling all these months. And when Derek had first mentioned the other woman, he'd spoken as though Reed and Danielle's relationship was a permanent one.

Danielle and Ellen couldn't have been more different. Ellen was practical and down-to-earth. She'd had to be. After her father's death, she'd become the cornerstone that held the family together.

Danielle, on the other hand, had obviously been pampered and indulged all her life. Ellen guessed that she'd been destined from birth to be a wealthy socialite, someone who might, in time, turn to charitable works to occupy herself. They were women with completely dissimilar backgrounds, she and Danielle. And completely different futures.

"I'll be in Georgia the latter part of next week," Reed was saying.

"You're full of good news, aren't you?"

"It's my work, Ellen," his soft voice accused her.

"I wasn't complaining. It just seems that the minute we come to an understanding, you're off again."

"It won't be long this time. A couple of days. I'll fly in for the meeting and be home soon afterward."

"You'll be here for Christmas?" Her thoughts flew to her family and how much she wanted each one of them to meet Reed. Bud, especially. Recently her brother's letters had revealed a new maturity. Bud would be in Yakima over the holidays and Ellen was planning to take the

Greyhound over to spend some time with him. But first she had to get through her exams.

"I'll be here."

"Good." But it was too soon to ask Reed to join her for the trip home. He might misinterpret her invitation, see something that wasn't there. She had no desire to pressure him into the sort of commitment that meeting her family might imply.

After their meal, they walked along the pier, holding hands. The evening air was chilly and Ellen shivered involuntarily. Reed wrapped his arm around her shoulder to lend her his warmth.

"I enjoyed tonight," he murmured.

"I did, too." She bent her arm so that her fingers linked with his.

"Tomorrow night—"

"No." She stopped him, turning so that her arm slid around his middle. Tilting her head back, she stared into the troubled green eyes. "Let's not talk about tomorrow. With us, it can only be one day at a time."

His mouth met hers before she could finish speaking. A gentle brushing of lips, a light exchange. Petal soft and petal smooth. Then he deepened the kiss, and his arms tightened around her, and her whole body hummed with joy.

Ellen was lost, irretrievably lost, in the taste and scent of this man. She felt frightened by her response to him—it would be so easy to lose her heart. But she couldn't let that happen. Not yet. It was too soon. Far too soon.

HER WORDS about taking each day as it comes were forcefully brought to Ellen's mind the following evening. She'd gone to the store and noticed Reed's Porsche parked in the driveway. When she returned, both Reed and the sports car had disappeared. Swallowing down the hurt, Ellen acknowledged that Reed was with Danielle.

CHAPTER SEVEN

"WHY COULDN'T I SEE THAT?" Ellen moaned, looking over the algebraic equation Reed had worked out. "If I can fix a stopped-up sink, tune a car engine and tie flies, why can't I understand something this simple?" She was at the end of her rope with this math class and quickly losing a grip on the more advanced theories they were now studying.

"Here, let me show it to you again."

Her hand lifted the bouncy curls off her forehead. "Do you think it'll do any good?"

"Yes, I do." Reed obviously had more faith in her powers of comprehension than she did. Step by step, he led her through another problem. When he explained the textbook examples, the whole process seemed so logical and simple. Yet when she set out to solve a similar equation, nothing went right.

"I give up." Throwing her hands over her head, she leaned back in the kitchen chair and groaned aloud. "I should have realized that algebra would be too much for me; I had difficulty memorizing the multiplication tables, for heaven's sake."

"What you need is a break."

"I couldn't agree more. Twenty years?" She stood up and brought the cookie jar to the table. "Here, this will help ease the suffering." She offered him a chocolate-chip cookie and took one herself. Reed's calm, assured attitude as he tutored her had been little short of amazing.

"Be more patient with yourself," he insisted.

"There's only three weeks left in this term. I haven't got time to mosey around and smell the cherry blossoms. I need to understand this stuff and I need to understand it now."

He laid his hands on her shoulders, massaging gently. "No, you don't. Come on, I'm taking you to a movie."

"I've got to study," she protested, but not too strenuously. Escaping for an hour or two sounded infinitely more appealing than struggling with these impossible equations.

"There's a wonderful foreign film showing at the Moore Egyptian Theater and we're going. We can worry about that assignment once we get back."

"But, Reed—"

"No buts. We're going." He took her firmly by the hand and led her into the front hall. Derek and Monte were watching TV and the staccato sounds of machine guns firing could be heard in the background. Neither boy noticed them until Reed opened the hall closet.

"Where are you two headed?" Derek asked, peering around the living-room door as Reed handed Ellen her jacket.

"A movie."

Instantly Derek muted the television. "The two of you alone? Together?"

"I imagine there will be one or two others at the theater," Reed responded dryly.

"Can I come?" Monte had joined Derek in the doorway and he clearly had no qualms about inviting himself along.

Instantly Derek's elbow shoved the other boy in the ribs. "On second thought, just bring me back some popcorn, okay?"

"It's yours."

Ellen pulled a knit cap over her ears. "Do either of you want anything else? I'd buy out the concession stand if one of you felt inclined to do my algebra."

"No way."

"Bribing them won't help," Reed commented, reaching for her hand.

"I know, but I was hoping."

It was a cold, blustery night. An icy north wind whipped against them as they hurried to Reed's truck. He opened the door for her before running around to the driver's side.

"Brr." Ellen stuffed her hands inside her jacket pockets. "If I doubted it was winter before, now I know."

"Come here and I'll warm you." He patted the seat beside him, indicating that she should slide closer.

Willingly she complied, until she sat so near to him that her thigh was pressing softly against his. Neither of them moved. Reed's right hand rested on the ignition key. It had been several days since they'd been completely alone together and longer still since he'd held or kissed her without interruption. The past ten days had been filled with frustration. Often she'd noticed Reed's gaze on her, studying her face and her movements, and she'd felt his angry disappointment. It seemed that every time he touched her one of the boys would unexpectedly appear.

Reed dropped his hand from the key and he turned to her. Their thoughts echoed each other's; their eyes locked hungrily. Ellen required no invitation. She'd been longing for his touch for days. With a tiny cry she reached for him just as his arms came out to encircle her, drawing her even closer.

"This is crazy," he whispered fervently into her hair.

"I know."

"I've been wanting to hold you for days." As though he couldn't deny himself any longer, his hands cradled her face and he slowly lowered his mouth to hers. His lips skimmed lightly, tenderly, over hers, torturing her with anticipation.

"You do taste like cotton candy," he whispered.

Ellen was so consumed with longing that his words barely registered in her bemused mind. Her mouth and tongue melted against his like the sweetest of sugars.

"Reed," she groaned, arching closer.

Their lips clung and his tongue sought and found hers in a loving duel, dipping again and again to taste her sweetness. Reed's hand went around her ribs as he held her tight. The kiss was long and thoroughly satisfying.

Panting, he tore his mouth from hers and buried his face in the sloping curve of her neck. "We better get to that movie."

It was all Ellen could do to nod her head in agreement.

When Reed made a move to start the truck, she saw that his hand was trembling. She was shaking too, but no longer from cold. Reed had promised to warm her and he had, but not quite in the way she'd expected.

They were silent as Reed switched on the engine and pulled onto the street. After days of carefully avoiding any kind of touch, any lingering glances, they'd sat in the driveway kissing in direct view of curious eyes. She realized that the boys could easily have been watching them. Nothing made sense anymore.

Ellen felt caught up in a tide that tossed her closer and closer to a long stretch of rocky beach. Powerless to alter the course of her emotions, she feared for her heart, afraid of being caught in the strong pull of the undertow.

"The engineering department is having a Christmas party this weekend at the Space Needle," Reed murmured.

Ellen nodded. Twice in the past week he'd left the house wearing formal evening clothes. He hadn't told her where he was going, but she knew. He'd driven the Porsche and he'd come back smelling of expensive perfume. For a Christmas party with his peers, Reed would escort Danielle. She understood that and tried to accept it.

"I want you to come with me."

"Reed," she breathed, uncertain. "Are you sure?"

"Yes," his hand reached for hers and squeezed. "I want you with me."

"The boys—"

"To hell with the boys. I'm tired of playing cat and mouse games with them."

Her smile came from her heart, radiating through her eyes. "I am too."

"I'm going to have a long talk with them."

"Don't," she pleaded. "It isn't necessary to say anything."

"They'll start in with their insufferable teasing."

"Let them, and then we can say something. I don't want to invite trouble."

He frowned briefly. "All right."

The Moore Egyptian was located in the heart of downtown Seattle, so parking was limited. They finally found a spot on the street three blocks away. They left the truck and hurried through the cold, arm in arm, not talking much. The French film was a popular one; by the time they reached the theater, a long line had already formed outside.

A blast of wind sliced through Ellen's jacket and she buried her hands in her pockets. Reed leaned close to ask her something, then paused, slowly straightening.

"Morgan." A tall, brusque-looking man approached Reed.

"Hello, Dailey," Reed said, quickly stepping away from Ellen.

"I wouldn't have expected to see you out on a night like this," the man Reed had called Dailey was saying.

"This film is supposed to be good."

"I've heard that too." Dailey's eyes returned to the line and rested on Ellen, seeking an introduction. Reed didn't give him one. It seemed as though Reed was pretending he wasn't with Ellen.

She offered the man a feeble smile, wondering why Reed would move away from her, why he wouldn't introduce her to his acquaintance. The line moved slowly toward the ticket booth and Ellen went with it, leaving Reed talking to Dailey on the sidewalk. Resentment flared when he rejoined her a few minutes later.

"That was a friend of a friend."

Ellen didn't answer him. Somehow she didn't believe him. And she resented the fact that he'd ignored the most basic of courtesies and left her standing on the sidewalk alone, while he spoke with a friend. The way he'd acted, anyone would assume Reed didn't want the man to know Ellen was with him. That hurt. Fifteen minutes earlier she'd been soaring with happiness at his unexpected invitation to the Christmas party, and now she was consumed with doubt and bitterness. Perhaps this Dailey was a friend of Danielle's and Reed didn't want the other woman to know he was out with Ellen. But that didn't really sound like Reed.

Once inside the theater, Reed bought a huge bucket of buttered popcorn. They located good seats, despite the crowd, and sat down, neither of them speaking. As the room darkened and the thick curtain parted, Reed placed his hand on the back of her neck.

Ellen stiffened. "Are you sure you want to do that?"

"What?"

"Touch me. Someone you know may recognize you."

"Ellen, listen . . ."

The credits started to roll on the huge screen and she shook her head, telling him she didn't want to hear any of his excuses. She sincerely doubted that he had one.

Maintaining her bad mood was impossible with the comedy that unraveled before them. Unable to stop herself, Ellen laughed until tears formed in the corners of her eyes; she was clutching her stomach because it hurt so much from laughing. Reed seemed just as amused as she was, and a couple of times during the film, their smiling gazes met. Before she knew it, Reed was holding her hand and she hadn't a thought of resisting when he draped his arm over her shoulder.

Afterward, as they strolled outside, he tucked her hand in the crook of his elbow. "I told you a movie would make you feel better."

It had and it hadn't. Yes, she'd needed the break, but Reed's behavior outside the theater earlier had revived the insecurities she was trying so hard to suppress. She knew she wasn't nearly as beautiful or sophisticated as Danielle. Nor did she possess the sterling social background of the other woman.

"You do feel better?" His finger lifted her chin to study her eyes.

She might have been confused, but there was no denying that the film had been wonderful. "I haven't laughed that hard in ages," she told him, smiling.

"Good."

FRIDAY NIGHT, Ellen wore her most elaborate outfit—black velvet pants and a silver lamé top. She'd spent hours debating whether an evening gown would have been more appropriate, but had finally decided on the pants. Examining herself from every direction in the full-length mirror that hung from her closet door, Ellen released a pent-up breath and closed her eyes. This one night, she wanted everything perfect. Her sling-back heels felt a little uncomfortable, but she'd get used to them. She rarely had any reason to wear heels. She'd chosen them now because Reed had said there would be dancing and she wanted to adjust her height to his.

By the time she reached the foot of the stairs, Reed was waiting for her. His eyes softened as he gazed at her, taking in everything; from her shining curls to her elegant shoes. "You're lovely."

"Oh Reed, are you sure? I don't mind changing if you'd rather I didn't wear pants."

His eyes held hers in a lengthy, intimate exchange. "I don't want you to change a thing."

"Hey, Ellen." Derek burst out of the kitchen, and stopped abruptly. "Wow." For an instant he looked as though he'd lost his breath. "Hey, guys," he called eagerly. "Come and look at Ellen."

The other two joined Derek. Pat dropped his basketball to the carpet, where it bounced once and rolled away. "Gee, you look like a movie star."

Monte closed his mouth and opened it again. His Adam's apple bobbed up and down his throat. "You're *pretty*."

"Don't sound so shocked."

"It's just that we've never seen you dressed...like this," Pat mumbled.

"Are you going out with Charlie?"

Ellen glanced at Reed, suddenly unsure. She hadn't dated Charlie in weeks. She hadn't wanted to.

"She's going out with me," Reed explained in an even voice that didn't invite comment.

"With you? Where?" Derek's eyes got that mischievous twinkle Ellen recognized so readily.

"A party."

"What about—" He stopped suddenly, swallowing several times.

"You wanted to comment on something?" Reed encouraged dryly.

"I thought I was going to say something," Derek muttered, clearly embarrassed, "but then I realized I wasn't."

"Good." Hiding a smile, Reed held Ellen's coat for her.

She slipped her arms into the satin-lined sleeves and reached for her beaded bag. "Good night, boys, and don't wait up."

"Right." Monte raised his index finger. "We won't wait up."

Derek took a step forward. "Should I say anything to someone...anyone...in case either of you gets a phone call?"

"Try hello," Reed answered, shaking his head.

"Right." Derek stuck his hand inside his pants pocket. "Have a good time."

"We intend to."

Ellen managed to hold back her laughter until they were on the front porch. But when the door clicked shut the giggles escaped and she pressed a hand to her mouth. "Derek thought he was going to say something."

"Then he realized he wasn't," Reed finished for her, chuckling. His hand at her elbow guided her down the steps. "They're right about one thing. You do look exceptionally lovely tonight."

"Thank you, but I hadn't thought it would be such a shock."

"The problem is the boys are used to seeing you as a substitute mother. It's suddenly dawned on them what an attractive woman you are."

"And how was it you noticed?"

He studied her a moment, his gaze caressing and ardent. "The day I arrived and found you in my kitchen wearing only a bra, I knew."

"I was wearing more than that," she argued.

"Maybe, but at the time that was all I saw." He stroked her cheek with the tip of his finger, then firmly tucked her arm in his.

Ellen felt a sense of warm contentment as Reed led her to the sports car. This night would be one she'd treasure all her life. She realized it as surely as she recognized that somewhere in the past two weeks Reed had made an unconscious decision about their relationship. Maybe she was being silly in judging the strength of their bond by what car he chose to drive. And maybe not. Reed was escorting her to this party in his Porsche because he viewed her in a new light. He saw her now as a beautiful, alluring woman—no longer as the independent college student who seemed capable of mastering everything but algebra.

The Space Needle came into view as Reed pulled onto
Denny Street. The world-famous Needle, which had been
built for the 1962 World's Fair, rose 605 feet above the
Seattle skyline. Ellen had taken the trip up to the observation deck only once and she'd been thrilled at the
unobstructed view of the Olympic and Cascade moun-
tain ranges. Looking out at the unspoiled beauty of Puget
Sound, she'd understood immediately why Seattle was
described as one of the world's most livable cities.

For this evening, Reed explained, his office had
booked the convention rooms on the hundred-foot level
of the Needle. The banquet facilities had been a recent
addition, and Ellen wondered what sort of view would be
available.

As Reed eased to a stop in front of the Needle, a red-
coated valet suddenly appeared, opening Ellen's door,
offering her his gloved hand. She climbed as gracefully
as she could from the low-built vehicle. Her smile felt a
little strained, and she took a deep breath to dispel the
gathering tension. She wanted everything about the evening to be perfect; she longed for Reed to be proud of
her, to feel that she belonged in his life—and in his world.

Her curiosity about the view was answered as soon as
they stepped from the elevator into the large circular
room. She glanced at the darkened sky that resembled
folds of black velvet, sprinkled with glittering gems.
When she had a chance she'd walk over toward the windows. For now, she was more concerned with fitting into
Reed's circle and being accepted by his friends and colleagues.

Bracing herself for the inevitable round of introduc-
tions, she scanned the crowd for the man she'd seen outside the theater. He didn't seem to be at the party and
Ellen breathed easier. If Dailey was there, he would surely

make a comment about seeing her with Reed that night, and she wouldn't know how to answer him.

As they made their way through the large room, several people called out to Reed. When he introduced Ellen, two or three of them appeared to have trouble concealing their surprise that he wasn't with Danielle. But after only a few seconds of embarrassment, the moment she'd dreaded most had passed. No one mentioned Danielle and they all seemed to accept Ellen freely, although a couple of people tossed her curious looks. Eventually, Ellen breathed easier and smiled up at Reed, her heart in her eyes.

"That wasn't so bad, was it?" he asked, his voice tender.

"Not at all."

"Would you like something to drink?"

"Please." A drink didn't sound particularly appealing just then, but at least it would give her something to do with her hands.

"I'll be right back."

Ellen watched Reed cross the room toward the bar, proud of the fine figure he cut. He wore the suit with an easy assurance, completely unaware of how splendid he looked. Ellen was absurdly proud of him and made no attempt to disguise her feelings when he returned to her, carrying two glasses of white wine.

"You shouldn't look at me like that," he murmured handing her a glass.

"Why?" she teased, her eyes sparkling. "Does it embarrass you?"

"No. It makes me wish I could ignore everyone in this room and kiss you, right this minute." The slow, almost boyish grin spread across his features.

"That would certainly cause quite a stir."

"But not half the commotion if you knew what else I was thinking."

"Oh?" She hid a smile by taking another sip of wine.

"Are we back to that word again?"

"Just what do you have in mind?"

He dipped his head so that he appeared to be whispering something in her ear, though actually his lips brushed her face. "I'll show you later."

"I'll be waiting."

They stood together, listening to the music and the laughter. Ellen found it curious that he'd introduced her to so few people and then only to those who'd approached him. But she dismissed her qualms as petty, and worse, paranoid. After all, she told herself, she was here to be with Reed, not to make small talk with his friends.

He finished his drink and suggested another. While he returned to the bar for refills, Ellen wandered through the crowd, seeking her way to the windows for a glimpse of the magnificent view. But as she moved, she kept her gaze trained on Reed.

A group of men stopped him, questioning him animatedly. His head was inclined toward them, and he appeared to be giving them his rapt attention. Yet periodically his gaze would flicker through the crowd, searching for her. When he located her by the huge floor-to-ceiling windows, he smiled as though he felt relieved. With an abruptness that bordered on rudeness, he excused himself from the group and strolled in her direction.

"I didn't see where you'd gone."

"I wasn't about to leave you," she told him. Turning, she faced the window, watching the lights of the ferry boats glide across the dark-green waters of Puget Sound.

His hands rested on her shoulders and Ellen leaned back against him, warmed by his nearness. "It's lovely from up here."

"Exquisite," he agreed, his mouth close to her ear. "But I'm not talking about the view." His hands slid lazily down her arms. "Dance with me," he said, taking her hand and leading her to the dance floor.

Ellen walked obediently into his arms, loving the feel of being close to Reed. She pressed her cheek against the smooth fabric of his dark jacket as they swayed gently to the slow, dreamy music.

"I don't normally do a lot of dancing," he whispered.

Ellen wouldn't have guessed that. He moved with an unexpected grace. She assumed that he'd escorted Danielle around a dance floor more than once during the course of their relationship. At the thought of the other woman, Ellen grew uneasy, but she forced her tense body to relax. Reed had chosen to bring her, and not Danielle, to this party. That had to mean something—something wonderful and exciting.

"Dancing was just an excuse to hold you."

"You don't need an excuse," she whispered in return.

"In a room full of people, I do."

"Shall we wish them away?" She closed her eyes, savoring the feel of his hard, lithe body pressing against her own.

He maneuvered them into the darkest corner of the dance floor and immediately claimed her mouth in a shattering kiss that sent her world spinning into orbit. His fingers sank into the thick curls at her nape, and his tongue chased hers.

Mindless of where they were, Ellen arched upward, Reed responded by sliding his hands down her back, down to her hips, drawing her even closer.

Roughly he dragged his mouth across her cheek. "I'm sorry we came."

"Why?"

"I don't want to waste time with all these people around. We're so seldom alone. I want you, Ellen."

His honest, straightforward statement sent the fire roaring through her veins. "I know. I want you, too." Her voice was unsteady. "But it's a good thing we aren't alone together very often." At the rate things were progressing between them, Ellen felt, for once, relieved that the boys were at the house. Otherwise, it would have been impossible to leave Reed and go up to her room alone....

"Hey, Reed." A friendly voice boomed out only a few feet away. "Aren't you going to introduce me to your friend?"

Reed stiffened and for a moment Ellen wondered if he was going to pretend he hadn't heard. He looked at her through half-closed eyes, and she grinned up at him, mutely telling him she didn't mind. Their private world couldn't last forever. She knew that. They were at a party, an office party and Reed was expected to mingle with his colleagues.

"Hello, Ralph." Reed's arm slid around Ellen's waist, keeping her close.

"Hello there." But Ralph wasn't watching Reed. "Well, good buddy, aren't you going to introduce me?"

"Ellen Cunningham, Ralph Forester."

Ralph extended his hand and captured Ellen's in both of his for a long moment. His eyes were frankly admiring.

"I don't suppose you'd let me steal this beauty away for a dance, would you?" Although the question was directed to Reed, Ralph didn't take his eyes from Ellen. "Leave it to you to be with the most beautiful woman here," the other man teased. "You attract them like flies."

Reed's hand tightened around Ellen, pinching her waist, but she was convinced he wasn't aware of it. "Ellen?" He left the choice to her.

"I don't mind." She glanced at Reed and noted that his expression was carefully blank. But she knew him too well to be fooled. She could see that his jaw was rigid with tension and that his eyes revealed sharp annoyance at the other man's intrusion. Gradually he lowered his arm, releasing her.

Ralph stepped forward and claimed Ellen's hand, leading her onto the dance floor.

She swallowed tightly as she placed her left hand on his shoulder and her right hand in his. Wordlessly they moved to the soft music. But when Ralph tried to bring her closer, Ellen resisted.

"Have you known Reed long?" Ralph asked then, his hand trailing sensuously up and down her back.

She tensed, holding herself stiffly. "Several months now." Despite her efforts to keep her voice even and controlled, she sounded slightly breathless.

"How'd you meet?"

"Through his brother." The less said about their living arrangements, the better. Ellen could just guess what Ralph would say if he knew they were living in the same house. "Do you two work together?"

"For the last six years," the other man declared, studying her curiously.

They whirled around and Ellen caught a glimpse of Reed standing against the opposite wall, studying them like a hawk zeroing in on its prey before swooping down to make the kill. Ralph apparently noticed Reed as well.

"I don't think Reed was all that anxious to have you dance with me."

"I'm sure it doesn't matter."

Ralph chortled gleefully, obviously enjoying Reed's reaction. "Not if the looks he's giving me are any indication. I can't believe it. Reed Morgan is jealous," he said with another chuckle, leading her out of Reed's sight and into the dimly lit center of the floor.

"I'm sure you're mistaken."

"Well, look at him."

All Ellen could see was Reed peering suspiciously at them across the crowded dance floor.

Ralph seemed overjoyed at Reed's behavior. "This is too good to be true."

"What do you mean?"

"There isn't a woman in our department who wouldn't give her eyeteeth to go out with Reed."

Ellen was shocked, yet somehow unsurprised. "Oh?"

"Half the women there are in love with him and he ignores them. He's friendly, don't get me wrong. But it's all business. Every time a single woman gets transferred into our area it takes a week, maybe two, for her to fall for Reed. The rest of us guys just stand back and shake our heads. But with Reed otherwise occupied, we might have a chance."

"He *is* wonderful," Ellen admitted, managing to keep a courteous smile on her face. What Ralph was describing sounded so much like her own feelings that she couldn't doubt the truth of what he said.

Ralph arched his thick brows and studied her. "You too?"

"I'm afraid so."

"What's this guy got?" He sighed expressively, shaking his head. "Is it bottled?"

"Unfortunately, I don't think so," Ellen responded lightly, liking Ralph more and more. His approach might have been a bit overpowering at first, but he was honest and compelling in his own right. "I don't imagine you have much trouble with the ladies."

"As long as I don't bring them around Reed, I'm fine." A smile swept his face. "The best thing that could happen would be if he were to marry. I don't suppose that's in the offing between you two?"

He was so blithely serious that Ellen laughed. "Sorry."

"You're sure?"

Ralph was probably referring to some rumor he'd heard about Danielle. "There's another woman he's seeing. They've known each other for a long time and apparently, they're fairly serious," she explained, keeping her voice calmly detached.

"I don't believe it," Ralph countered, frowning. "Reed wouldn't be tossing daggers at my back if he was involved with someone else. One thing I suspect about this guy, he's a one-woman man."

Ellen closed her eyes, trying to shut out the small pain that came from the direction of her heart. She didn't know what to believe about Reed anymore. All she could do was hold on to the moment. Wasn't that what she'd told him earlier—that they'd have to take things day by day? She didn't want to read too much into his actions. She couldn't. She was on the brink of falling in love with him...if she hadn't already. To allow herself to think that he might feel the same way was surely asking for trouble. For heartbreak.

The music ended and Ralph gently let her go. "I'd best return you to Reed or he's likely to come after me."

"Thank you for...everything."

"You're welcome, Ellen." With one hand at the back of her waist, he steered her toward Reed.

They were within a few feet of him when Danielle suddenly appeared. She seemed to have come out of nowhere. "Reed!" She was laughing delightedly, flinging herself into his arms and kissing him intimately. "Oh, darling, you're so right. Being together is more important than any ski trip. I'm so sorry. Will you forgive me?"

CHAPTER EIGHT

"ELLEN," RALPH ASKED. "Are you all right?"

"I'm fine," she lied.

"Sure you are," he mocked, sliding his arm around her waist and guiding her back to the dance floor. "I take it the blonde is Woman Number One?"

"You got it." The anger was beginning to build inside her. "Beautiful too, you'll notice."

"Well, you aren't exactly chopped liver."

She gave a small, mirthless laugh. "Nice of you to say so, but in comparison, I come in a poor second."

"I wouldn't say that."

"Then why can't you take your eyes off Danielle?"

"Danielle. Hmm." He dragged his gaze away from the other woman and stared blankly into Ellen's round eyes. "Sorry." For her part, Ellen instinctively turned her back to Reed, unable to bear the sight of him holding and kissing another woman.

"Someone must have gotten their wires crossed."

"Like me," Ellen muttered. She'd been an idiot to assume that Reed had meant anything by his invitation. He'd just needed someone to escort to this party, she fumed, and his first choice hadn't been available. She was a substitute, and a poor one at that.

"What do you want to do?"

Ellen frowned, her thoughts fragmented. "I don't know yet. Give me a minute to think."

"You two could always fight for him."

"The stronger woman takes the spoils? No, thanks. I'm not much into mud wrestling." Despite herself she laughed. It certainly would have created a diversion at this formal, rather staid party.

Craning his neck, Ralph peered over at the other couple. "Reed doesn't seem too pleased to see her."

"I can imagine. The situation has put him in a bit of a bind."

"I admit it's unpleasant for you, but, otherwise, I'm enjoying this immensely."

Who wouldn't? The scene was just short of being comical. "I thought you said Reed was a one-woman man."

"I guess I stand corrected."

Ellen was making a few corrections herself, revising some cherished ideas about a certain Reed Morgan.

"I don't suppose you'd consider staying with me the rest of the evening?" Ralph suggested hopefully.

"Consider it? It'd say it was the best offer I've had in weeks." She might feel like a fool, but she didn't plan to hang around here looking like one.

Ralph nudged her and bent his head to whisper in her ear, "Reed's staring at us. And he doesn't look pleased."

With a determination born of anger and pride, she forced a smile to her lips and gazed adoringly up at Ralph. "How am I doing?" she asked, batting her thick lashes at him.

"Wonderful, wonderful." He swung her energetically around to the beat of the music. "Uh-oh, here he comes."

Reed weaved his way through the dancing couples and tapped Ralph on the shoulder. "I'm cutting in."

Ellen tightened her grip on Reed's colleague, silently pleading with him to stay. "Sorry, old buddy, but Ellen's with me now that your lady friend has arrived."

"Ellen?" Reed's eyes narrowed as he stared intently into hers. The other dancing couples were waltzing around and glancing curiously at the party of three that had formed in the center of the room.

She couldn't remember ever seeing anyone look more furious than Reed did at this moment. "Maybe I'd just better leave," she said in a low, faltering voice.

"I'll take you home," Ralph offered, dropping his hand to her waist.

"You came with me. You'll leave with me." Reed grasped her hand, pulling her toward him.

"Obviously you made provisions," Ellen countered, "just on the off chance Danielle showed up. How else did she get in here?"

"How the hell am I supposed to know? She probably told the manager she was with me."

"And apparently she is," Ellen hissed.

"Maybe Reed and I should wrestle to decide the winner," Ralph suggested, glancing at Ellen and sharing a comical grin.

"Maybe."

Clearly, Reed saw no humor in the situation. Anger darkened his handsome face, and a muscle twitched in his jaw as the tight rein on his patience slipped.

Ralph withdrew his hand. "Go ahead and dance. It's obvious you two have a lot to talk about."

Reed took Ellen in his arms, his grip rough and almost painful.

"You're hurting," she cried.

His hold instantly relaxed. "I suppose you're furious."

"Have I got anything to be angry about?" Now that the initial shock had worn off, and the anger had dissipated, she was beginning to find some humor in the situation.

"Hell, yes. But I want a chance to explain."

"Don't bother. I've got the picture."

"And I'm sure you don't." His eyes demanded that she look up at him.

Ellen stubbornly refused for as long as she could, but the pull of his gaze was too compelling to resist. "It doesn't matter. Ralph said he'd take me home and . . ."

"I've already explained my feelings on that subject."

"Wonderful, Reed. Your Porsche seats two. Is Danielle supposed to sit on my lap?"

"She came uninvited. Let her find her own way home."

"You don't mean that."

"The hell I don't."

"You can't do that to Danielle. It would humiliate her." Ellen didn't bother to mention what it was doing to her.

"She deserves it."

"Reed, no." Her hold on his forearm tightened. "This is unpleasant enough for all of us. Don't complicate it."

The song ended and the music faded from the room. Reed fastened his hand on Ellen's elbow, guiding her across the floor to where Danielle was standing with Ralph. The two were sipping champagne.

"Hello again," Ellen began amicably, doing her utmost to appear friendly, trying to smooth over an already awkward situation.

"Hello." Danielle stared at her curiously, obviously not recognizing Ellen.

"You remember Ellen Cunningham, don't you?" Reed stated dryly.

"Not that college girl your brother invited—" Danielle stopped abruptly, shock etched starkly on her perfect features. "You're Ellen Cunningham?"

"In the flesh." Still trying to keep things light, she cocked her head toward Ralph and spoke stagily out of the side of her mouth, turning the remark into a farcical aside. "I wasn't at my sterling best when we met the first time."

"You were fiddling around with that electrical outlet and Reed was horrified," Danielle inserted, her voice completely humorless, her eyes narrowed assessingly. "You didn't even look like a girl."

"She does now." Ralph beamed her a brilliant smile.

"Yes." Danielle swallowed, her face puckered with concern. "She looks very...nice."

"Thank you." Ellen dipped her head.

"I've made a terrible mess of things," Danielle continued, casually handing her half-empty glass to a passing waiter. "Reed mentioned the party weeks ago and Mom and I had this ski party planned. I told him I couldn't attend and then I felt terribly guilty because Reed's been such an angel escorting me to all the charity balls."

Ellen didn't hear a word of explanation beyond the fact that Reed had originally asked Danielle to the party. The other woman had just confirmed Ellen's suspicions, and the hurt went through her like a thousand needles. He'd invited her only because Danielle couldn't attend.

"There's no problem," Ellen said in a colorless voice. "I understand how these things happen. He asked you first; you stay and I'll leave."

"I couldn't do that."

Reed's eyes were saying the same thing. Ellen ignored him, and she ignored Danielle. Slipping her hand around Ralph's arm, she looked up at him and smiled, silently thanking him for being her friend. "It isn't any problem, I assure you. Ralph's been wonderful."

Reed's expression was impassive, almost aloof, as she swung around to look at him. "I'm sure you won't mind if Ralph takes me home."

"How understanding of you," Danielle simpered, locking her arm around Reed's.

"It's no problem. I'd much prefer this to mud wrestling."

"Mud wrestling?" Danielle clapped her hands with delight. "What a bizarrely fascinating idea."

Ralph choked on a swallow of his drink, his face turning several shades of red as he struggled to hide his amusement. The only one who revealed no sense of humor was Reed, whose face grew more and more shadowed.

The band struck up a lively song and the dance floor quickly filled. "Come on, Reed," Danielle said, her blue eyes eager. "Let's dance." Leading the way, she tugged at Reed's hand and gave a sensuous little wriggle of her hips. "You know how much I love to boogie."

So Reed had done his share of dancing with Danielle—probably at all those charity balls she'd mentioned. Ellen had guessed as much and yet he'd tried to give her the impression that he rarely danced.

But examining the stiff way Reed held himself now, Ellen could almost believe him.

Ralph placed a gentle hand on her shoulder. "I don't know about you, but I'm ready to get out of here."

Watching Reed hold Danielle in his arms was absurdly painful; her throat muscles constricted in an effort to hold back tears and she simply nodded her agreement.

"Did you have dinner? I'm starved."

Ellen blinked. Dinner. She couldn't remember. "No, I don't think... I'm not really hungry," she amended. The afternoon had been spent getting ready for the party, and she hadn't thought about food, assuming they'd have something to eat later in the evening.

"Sure you're hungry," Ralph insisted. "We'll stop off at a nice restaurant before I drive you home. I know where Reed's place is, so I know where you live. Don't look so shocked. I figured it out from what you and Danielle were saying. But don't worry, I understand—impoverished students sharing a house, and all that. So, what do you say? We'll have dinner and get home two hours after Reed. That should set him thinking."

Ellen didn't feel in any mood to play games at Reed's expense. "That's not a good idea."

Ralph's jovial expression sobered. "You've got it bad."

"I'll be fine."

His fingers stroked the back of her neck. "I know you will. Come on, let's get out of here."

The night that had begun with such promise had evaporated so quickly, leaving a residue of uncertainties and suspicions. As they neared the house, her composure gradually crumpled until she was nervously twisting the delicate strap of her beaded evening bag over and over again between her fingers. To his credit, Ralph attempted to carry the conversation, but her responses became less and less animated. She just wanted to get home and bury her head in her pillow.

By the time Ralph pulled up in front of the Capitol Hill house, they were both silent.

"Would you like to come in for coffee?" she offered. The illusion she'd created earlier of flippant humor was gone now. She hurt, and every time she blinked, a picture of Danielle dancing with Reed came to her mind. How easy it was to visualize the other woman's arms around his neck, pressing her voluptuous body against his. The image tormented Ellen with every breath she drew.

"No, I think I'll make it an early night."

"Liar," she teased affectionately. "Thank you. I couldn't have done it without you."

"No problem. Listen, if you want a shoulder to cry on, I'm available."

She dropped her gaze to the tightly coiled strap of her bag. "I'm fine. Really."

Gently he patted her hand. "Somehow I don't quite believe that." Opening the door, he came around to her side and helped her out.

On the top step of the porch, Ellen softly kissed his cheek. "Thanks again."

"Good night, Ellen."

"'Night." She took out her keys and unlocked the front door. Pushing it open, she discovered that the house was oddly dark and oddly deserted. It was still relatively early and she'd have expected the boys to be around. But not having to make excuses to them was a blessing she wasn't about to question.

As she removed her coat and headed for the stairs, she noticed the shadows bouncing around the darkened living room. She walked over to investigate and, two steps into the room, caught the sound of soft romantic music drifting from the stereo. A flicker of candlelight could be seen from the formal dining room.

Ellen stood there paralyzed taking in the romantic scene before her. A bottle of wine and two glasses were set out on the coffee table. A gentle fire blazed in the brick fireplace. And the soft violin music seemed to assault her from all sides.

"Derek," she called out.

Silence.

"All right, Pat and Monte. I know you're out there someplace."

Silence.

"I'd suggest the three of you do away with this...stuff before Reed returns. He's with Danielle and not in any mood for games." With that, she marched up the stairs, uncaring if they heard her or not.

"With Danielle?" she heard a male voice shout after her.

"What happened?"

Ellen pretended not to hear.

THE MORNING SUN sneaked into her window, splashing the pillow where Ellen lay awake staring sightlessly at the ceiling. Sooner or later she'd have to get out of bed, but she couldn't see any reason to rush the process. Besides, the longer she stayed up here, the greater her chances of missing Reed. The unpleasantness of facing him wasn't going to vanish with time, but she might be able to postpone it for a morning. Although she had to wonder whether Reed was any more keen on seeing her than she was on seeing him. Anyway she could always kill time by dragging out her algebra books and studying for the exam—but that was almost as distasteful as facing Reed.

No, she decided suddenly, she'd stay in her room until she was weak with hunger. Checking her wristwatch, she figured that would be about another five minutes.

Someone knocked on her bedroom door. Sitting up, Ellen pulled the sheets over her breasts. "Who is it?" she called out, not particularly eager to talk to anyone.

Reed threw open the door and stalked inside. He stood in the middle of the room with his hands on his hips and barked, "Are you planning to stay up here the rest of your life?"

"The idea has distinct possibilities." She glared back at him, her eyes flashing with outrage and ill humor. "By the way, you'll note that I asked who was at the door. I didn't say, 'come in.'" Her voice rose to a mockingly high pitch. "You might have walked in on me when I was dressing."

A smile crossed his boyish mouth. "Is that an invitation?"

"Absolutely not." She rose to a kneeling position, taking the sheets and blankets with her. She pointed a finger in the direction of the door. "Would you kindly leave? I'd like to get dressed."

"Don't let me stop you."

"Reed, please," she said, irritably. "I'm not in any mood to exchange witticisms with you."

"I'm not leaving until we talk."

"Unfair. I haven't had my cup of tea and my mouth feels like the bottom of Puget Sound."

"All right," he agreed reluctantly. "I'll give you ten minutes."

"How generous of you."

"Considering my frame of mind since you walked out on me last night, I consider it most charitable of me."

"Walked out on you!" She flew off the bed. Her mouth dropped so wide open, she felt as though her chin had lost its support. "That's rich."

"Ten minutes," he repeated, his voice dropping low in warning.

The whole time Ellen was dressing, she fumed. Reed had some nerve accusing her of walking out on him. He obviously didn't have any idea what it had cost her to leave him at that party with Danielle. He was thinking only of his own feelings, showing no regard for hers. He hadn't even acknowledged that she'd swallowed her pride to save them all from an extremely embarrassing situation.

Four male faces met hers when she appeared in the kitchen. "Good morning," she said with false enthusiasm.

The three boys looked sheepishly away. "'Morning," they droned. Each found something at the table to occupy his hands. Pat examined the grooves on his basketball as though seeking some insidious leak. Monte read the back of the cereal box and Derek folded the front page of the paper, pretending to read it.

"Ellen and I'd like a few minutes of privacy," Reed announced, frowning at the three boys.

Derek, Monte and Pat stood up simultaneously.

"I don't know that there's anything we have to say that the boys can't hear," she contradicted.

The three youths reclaimed their chairs, looking with bright-eyed expectancy first to Reed and then to Ellen.

Reed's scowl deepened. "Can't you see that Ellen and I need to talk?" He pointedly directed his comment to the boys.

"There's nothing to discuss," Ellen insisted, pouring boiling water into the mug and dipping the tea bag in the water several times before tossing it in the garbage.

"Yes, there is," Reed countered.

"Maybe it would be best if we did leave," Derek hedged, noticeably uneasy with his brother's anger and Ellen's feigned composure.

"You walk out of this room and there will be no packed lunches next week," Ellen cried softly, leaning against the counter and sipping her tea.

"I'm staying." Monte crossed his arms over his chest as though preparing for a long standoff.

Ellen knew she could count on Monte; his stomach would always take precedence. Childishly, she flashed Reed a saucy grin. He wasn't going to bulldoze her into any confrontation.

"Either you're out of here *now*, or you won't have a place to *live* next week," Reed flared back. At Derek's smug expression, Reed added, "And that includes you, little brother."

The boys exchanged shocked glances. "Sorry, Ellen," Derek mumbled on his way out of the kitchen. "I told Michelle I'd be over in a few minutes anyway." Without another moment's hesitation, Reed's brother was out the door.

"Well?" Hands placed on his hips, Reed approached Monte and Pat.

"Yes, well...I guess maybe I should probably..." Pat looked to Ellen for guidance, his resolve wavering.

"Go ahead." She dismissed them both with a wave of her hand.

"Are you sure you want us to go?" Monte asked anxiously, glancing at Reed and back at Ellen again.

Ellen smiled her appreciation at this small display of mettle. "I'll be perfectly all right."

The sound of the door swinging back and forth echoed through the emptiness of the large kitchen. Ellen drew a deep, calming breath and turned to confront Reed, who didn't look all that pleased to have her alone now, though he'd certainly gone to some lengths to arrange it. His face was pinched, and fine lines etched his eyes and mouth. Either he'd had a late night or he hadn't slept at all. Ellen decided it must have been the former.

"Well, I'm here within ten minutes, just as you decreed. If you've got something to say, say it."

"Don't rush me," he snapped.

Crossing her arms over her chest, Ellen released an exaggerated sigh. "First you want to talk to me—then you're not sure. This sounds amazingly like someone who asked me to a party once. First he wanted me with him—then he didn't."

"I wanted you there last night."

"Was I talking about you?" she asked in mock innocence.

"You're not making this easy." He plowed his fingers through his hair, the awkward movement at odds with the self-control he usually exhibited.

"Listen," she breathed, casting her eyes down. "You don't need to explain anything. I have a fairly accurate picture of what happened."

"I doubt that." But he didn't elaborate.

"I can understand why you'd prefer Danielle's company."

"I didn't. That had to be one of the most awkward moments of my life. I wanted you—not Danielle."

Sure, she mused sarcastically. That was the reason he'd introduced her to so few people. She'd had plenty of time in the past twelve hours to think. If she hadn't been so blinded by the stars in her eyes, she would have figured it out sooner. Reed had taken her to his company's party and kept her shielded from the other guests; he hadn't wanted her talking to his friends and colleagues. At the time, she'd been highly complimented, assuming he wanted her all to himself. Now she understood the reason. The others knew he'd invited Danielle; they knew that Danielle usually accompanied him to these functions. The other woman had an official status in Reed's life; Ellen didn't.

"It wasn't your fault," she told him. "I understand what happened. Unfortunately, it was unavoidable."

"I'd rather Danielle had left instead of you." He walked to her side, deliberately taking the mug of tea from her hand and setting it on the counter. Slowly his arms came around her.

Ellen hadn't the will to resist. She closed her eyes as her arms reached around him, almost of their own accord. He felt so warm and vital.

"I want us to spend the day together."

Her earlier intention of studying for her algebra exam flew out the window at the mere mention of being with Reed. Despite all her hesitations, all her doubts and fears, she couldn't refuse this chance to be with him. Alone, the two of them. "All right," she answered softly.

"Ellen." His breath stirred the curls on the crown of her head. "There's something you should know."

"Hmm."

"I'm flying out tomorrow morning for two days."

Her eyes flew open. "How long?"

"Two days, but after that, I won't be leaving again until the Christmas holidays are over."

She answered him with a nod. Traveling was part of his job, and any woman in his life would have to accept that. She was touched that he felt so concerned for her. "That's fine," she whispered. "I understand."

Ellen couldn't fault Reed for the remainder of the weekend. Saturday afternoon, they went Christmas shopping at the Tacoma Mall. His choice of shopping area surprised her, since there were several in the immediate area, much closer than the forty-five-minute drive to Tacoma. But they had a good time, wandering from store to store. Before she knew it, Christmas would be upon them and this was the first opportunity she'd had to do any real shopping. With Reed's help, she picked out gifts for the boys and her brother.

"You'll like Bud," she told him, licking a chocolate ice-cream cone. They found a place to sit, with their packages gathered around them, and took a fifteen-minute break.

"I imagine I will." A flash of amusement lit his eyes, then he abruptly looked away.

Ellen lowered her ice-cream cone. "What's so funny? Have I got chocolate on my nose?"

"No."

"What, then?"

"You must have forgiven me for what happened at the party."

Her eyes narrowed. "What makes you say that?"

"The way you looked into the future and claimed I'd like your brother, as though you and I are going to have a long, meaningful relationship."

The ice cream suddenly became terribly important and Ellen licked away at it with an all-consuming energy. "I told you before that I feel things have to be one day at a time with us. There are too many variables in our...relationship." She waved the ice cream in his direction. "And I use that term loosely."

"There is a future for us."

"You seem mighty sure of yourself."

"I'm more certain of you." He said it so smoothly that Ellen wondered if she heard him right. She would have challenged his arrogant assumption, but just then, he glanced at his wristwatch and suggested a movie.

By the time they returned to the house it was close to midnight. He kissed her with a tenderness that somehow reminded her of an early-summer dawn, but his touch was as potent as a sultry August afternoon.

"Ellen?" he murmured into her hair.

"Hmm?"

"I think you'd better go upstairs now."

The warmth of his touch had melted away the last traces of icy reserve that the party had built around her fragile heart. She didn't want to leave him. "Why?"

His hands gripped her shoulders, pushing her apart from him, putting an arm's length between them. "Because if you don't leave now, I may climb those stairs with you."

At his straightforward, honest statement, Ellen swallowed and blinked twice. "I enjoyed today. Thank you, Reed." He dropped his arms and she placed a trembling hand on the railing. "Have a safe trip."

"I will." He took a step toward her. "I wish I didn't have to go." His hand cupped her chin and he drew her face toward his, claiming her mouth with a hunger that shook Ellen to the core. It took all her strength not to throw herself against him and wrap her arms around him again.

MONDAY AFTERNOON, when Ellen walked into the house after her classes, the three boys were waiting for her. They looked up at her with peculiar expressions on their faces, as though she were someone they'd never seen before and they couldn't understand how she'd wandered into their kitchen.

"All right, what gives?"

"Gives?" Derek asked.

"You've got that guilty look."

"*We're* not the guilty party," Pat announced.

"All right, you'd better let me know what's happened so I can deal with it before Reed gets back."

"You'll need to," Monte said, his hand on the kitchen door. He swung it open so that the dining-room table came into view. In the center of the table was the largest bouquet of red roses Ellen had ever seen.

Her breath got trapped in her lungs as the shocked gasp slid from the back of her throat.

"Who . . . who sent those?"

"We thought you'd want to know so we took the liberty of reading the card."

Their prying barely registered in her numbed brain as she walked slowly into the room and removed the small card pinned to the bright red ribbon. It could have been Bud—but he didn't have the kind of money to buy roses. And if he did, Ellen suspected he wouldn't get them for his sister.

"Reed did it," Pat inserted eagerly.

"Reed?"

"We were as surprised as you."

Her gaze fell to the tiny envelope. She removed the card, biting into her bottom lip when she read the message. *I miss you. Reed.*

"He said he misses you," Derek added.

"I see that."

"Good grief, he'll be back tomorrow. How can he possibly miss you in this short a time?"

"I don't know." Lovingly her finger caressed the petals of a dewy rosebud. They were so incredibly beautiful, but their message was far more dear.

"I bet this is his way of telling you he regrets what happened the night of the party," Derek murmured.

"Not that any of us actually knows what happened. We'd like to, you understand, but it'd be considered bad manners to ask," Pat explained. "That is, unless you'd like to share with us why he'd take you to the party and then come back alone."

"He didn't get in until three that morning, either." Monte said accusingly. "You aren't going to let him off so easy are you, Ellen?"

Bowing her head to smell the sweet fragrance, she closed her eyes. "Roses cover a multitude of sins."

"Reed's feeling guilty, I think," Derek said with authority. "But he cares, or else he wouldn't have gone to this much trouble."

"Maybe he just wants to keep the peace," Monte added as an afterthought. "My dad bought my mom flowers once for no apparent reason."

"We all live together. Reed's probably figured out that he had to do something if he wanted to maintain the status quo."

"Right," Ellen agreed tartly, scooping up the flowers to take to her room. Maybe it was selfish to deprive the boys of the flowers' beauty, but she didn't care. They had been meant for her, as a private memento from Reed, and having them close was a comfort.

THE FOLLOWING DAY, Ellen cut her last morning class, knowing that Reed's flight arrived around noon. She could ill afford to skip algebra, but it wouldn't have done her any good to stay. The entire class time would have been spent thinking about Reed—so it made more sense to hurry home.

She stepped off the bus a block from the house and even from that distance she could see his truck parked in the driveway. It was the first—and only—thing she noticed. She sprinted toward home and dashed up the front steps.

Flinging open the door, she called breathlessly, "Anyone home?"

Both Reed and Derek came out of the kitchen.

Her eyes met Reed's from across the room. "Hi," she said in a low, husky voice. "Welcome home."

He took a step toward her, his warm gaze holding hers.

Neither spoke as Ellen threw her books on the sofa and advanced toward him.

He caught her around the waist as though he'd been away for months instead of days, hugging her fiercely.

Ellen savored the warmth of his embrace, closing her eyes to the overwhelming emotion she suddenly felt. Reed was becoming far too important in her life. But she no longer had the power to resist him. If she ever had.

"His plane was right on time," Derek was saying. "And the airport was hardly busy."

Irritably, Reed tossed a look over his shoulder. "Little brother, get lost."

CHAPTER NINE

"I'VE GOT A PRACTICE GAME today," Pat said, his fork cutting into the syrup-laden pancakes. "Can you come?"

Ellen's eyes met Reed's in mute communication. No longer did they bother to hide their attraction to each other from the boys. They couldn't. "What time?"

"Six."

"I can be there."

"What about you, Reed?"

Reed wiped the corners of his mouth with the paper napkin. "Sorry, I've got a meeting. But I should be home in time for the victory celebration."

Ellen thrilled to the way the boys automatically linked her name and Reed's. It had been that way from the time he'd returned from his short trip. But then, they'd given the boys plenty of reason to think of her and Reed as a couple. He and Ellen were with each other every free moment, the time they spent together was exclusively theirs. And Ellen loved it that way. She loved Reed, she loved being with him . . . and she loved every single thing about him. Almost. His reticence on the subject of Danielle had her a little worried, but she pushed it to the back of her mind. She couldn't bring herself to question him; she'd just have to assume that the earlier relationship was over now. As far as she knew, Reed hadn't spoken to Danielle since the night of the Christmas party. Even stronger evidence was the fact that he drove his truck every day. The Porsche sat parked in the garage, gathering dust.

Reed stood up and delivered his breakfast plate to the sink. "Ellen, walk me to the door?"

"Sure."

"For Pete's sake, the door's only two feet away," Derek scoffed, feeling noticeably brave. "You travel all over the world and all of a sudden you need someone to show you the way to the back door."

Ellen didn't see the look the two brothers exchanged, but Derek's mouth curved upward into a knowing grin. "Oh, I get it. Hey, guys, they want to be alone a minute. If we were a bit more into this romance thing we would have recognized it sooner."

"Just a minute." Monte wolfed down the last of his breakfast, still chewing as he carried his plate to the counter.

Ellen was mildly surprised that Reed didn't comment on Derek's needling, but she supposed they were becoming accustomed to it.

One by one, the boys left the kitchen. Silently, Reed stood by the back door, waiting. When the last one had departed, he slipped his arms around Ellen.

"You're getting mighty brave," she whispered, smiling into his intense green eyes. Lately, Reed seemed almost to invite the boys' comments. And when they responded, the teasing rolled off his back like rain off a well-waxed car.

"If you knew what I was thinking you'd be in the other room with Derek and the others." He slid a hand around the back of her neck and into her hair.

"Oh?" Despite her efforts not to blush, Ellen felt her face grow warm.

"It's torture being around you every day and not touching you," he said as his mouth inched closer to hers. "But it's a sweet torment," he concluded just before his mouth descended on hers in an excruciatingly slow kiss that seemed to melt Ellen's very bones.

Reality seemed light-years away as she clung to him, and she struggled to recover her equilibrium. "Reed," she pleaded, "you've got to get to work."

"Right." But he didn't stop kissing her and his grip seemed to tighten, arching her closer and closer.

"And I've got class." If he didn't stop soon, they'd both reach the point of no return. Each time he held and kissed her, it became more and more difficult to break away.

His hand cupped the throbbing fullness of her breast. His thumb teased her nipple to a hard peak and Ellen moaned. "Reed..."

"I know. I know." His throaty voice echoed through the fog that held her captive. "Now isn't the time or the place."

Her arms around his middle tightened as she burrowed her face against the hard muscles of his chest. With one heartbeat, she was telling Reed they had to stop and with the next, she refused to release him.

"I'll be late tonight," he murmured into her hair.

"Okay." She remembered that he'd told Pat something about a meeting.

"Let's go out to dinner." His warm breath fanned her temple. "Just the two of us, alone. I've come to love being alone with you."

Ellen wanted to cry with frustration. "I can't. Exams start next week and I've got to study."

"Need any help?"

"Only one subject." She looked up at him and sadly shook her head. "I don't suppose you can guess which one."

"Aren't you glad you've got me?"

"Eternally grateful." Ellen would never have believed that algebra could be her greatest downfall and her greatest ally. If it weren't for that one subject, she wouldn't have had the excuse to sit down with Reed every night to sort through her homework problems. But then, lately, she hadn't needed an excuse.

"We'll see how grateful you are when grades come out."

"I hate to disappoint you, but it's going to take a lot more than your excellent tutoring to rescue me from my fate this time." The exam was crucial. If she didn't do well, she would probably end up repeating the class. The thought filled her with dread. It would be a waste of her time and, even worse, a waste of precious funds.

Reed kissed her lightly before reluctantly releasing her. "Have a good day."

"You, too." She stood at the door until he'd climbed inside the pickup and waved to him when he backed out of the driveway.

Knowing she'd best get the stars out of her eyes before she had to confront the boys, Ellen loaded the dirty dishes into the dishwasher and cleaned off the counter, humming as she worked.

One of the boys knocked on the door. "Is it safe to come in yet?"

"Come on in. I'm waiting."

All three innocently strolled into the kitchen. "You and Reed are getting a little thick, aren't you?"

Running hot tap water into the sink, Ellen nodded. "I suppose."

"Reed hasn't seen Danielle in a long time."

Ellen didn't comment, but she did feel encouraged that Derek's conclusion was the same as hers.

"You know what I think?" he asked, hopping onto the counter so she was forced to look at him.

"I can only guess."

"I think Reed's getting serious about you."

"That's nice."

"*Nice*—is that all you can say?" He gave her a look of disgust. "That's my brother you're talking about. He could have any woman he wanted."

"I know." Coyly, she smiled at him as she poured soap into the dishwasher, then closed the door and turned the dial. Instantly the sound of rushing water could be heard, drowning out Derek's next comment.

"Sorry, I've got to get to class. I'll talk to you later." Still humming, she sauntered past Pat and Monte, offering them a friendly smile.

"She's got it bad." Ellen heard Monte comment. "She hardly even bakes anymore. Remember how she used to make cookies and cakes every week?"

"I didn't know love did that to a person," Pat grumbled.

"I'm not sure I like Ellen in love," Monte flung after her as she stepped out the door.

"I just hope she doesn't get hurt."

The boy's remarks echoed in her mind as the day wore on. Ellen didn't need to hear their doubts; she had more than enough of her own. Sudden qualms assailed her heart when she least expected it—like during algebra class, or during the long afternoon that followed.

But one look at Reed that evening and all her anxieties evaporated. As soon as she entered the house, she walked straight into the living room, hoping to find him there, and she did.

He folded the newspaper when she walked in. "How was the game?"

"Pat scored seventeen points and is a hero. Unfortunately, the Huskies lost." Sometimes, that was just the way life went: winning small victories yet losing the war.

"Something smells good." Monte followed her into the kitchen, sniffing appreciatively.

"There's a roast in the oven and an apple pie on the counter," she answered him, trading her coat for a terry-cloth apron. She'd bought the pie in hopes of celebrating the Huskies' victory. Now it would soothe their loss. "I imagine everyone's starved."

"I am," Monte announced.

"That goes without saying," Reed called from the living room, picking up the newspaper again.

Ellen checked the oven, shocked to discover that her hands were trembling. It was unfair that just seeing Reed would have this effect on her. As Monte had declared earlier in the day, she had it bad.

The evening was spent at the kitchen table, poring over her textbooks. Reed came in twice to make her a fresh cup of tea. Standing behind her chair, he glanced over her shoulder at the psychology book.

"Do you want me to get you anything?" she asked. This was the second time he'd strolled into the kitchen. She was studying there, rather than in her room, just to be close to Reed. Admittedly, her room offered more seclusion, but she preferred being around people—one person, actually.

"I don't need a thing." He kissed the top of her head. "And if I did, I'd get it myself. You study."

"Thanks."

"When's the first exam?"

"Monday."

He nodded. "You'll do fine."

"I don't want fine," she countered nervously. "I want fantastic."

"Then no doubt you'll do fantastic."

"Where are the boys?" The house was uncommonly silent for a weekday evening.

"Studying. I'm pleased to see they're taking exams as seriously as you are."

"We have to," she mumbled, her gaze dropping to her notebook.

"All right. I get the message. I'll quit pestering you."

"You're not pestering me."

"Right." He bent his head to kiss the side of her neck as his fingers sensuously stroked her arms.

Shivers raced down her spine and Ellen closed her eyes, unconsciously swaying toward him. "Now...now you're pestering me."

He chuckled, leaving her alone at the kitchen table when she would so much rather have had him with her every minute of every day.

THE FOLLOWING MORNING, Ellen stood by the door, watching Reed pull out of the driveway.

"Why do you do that?" Pat questioned, giving her a glance that said she looked utterly foolish standing there.

"Do what?" She decided the best reaction was to pretend that she didn't have the foggiest notion what he was talking about.

"Watch Reed leave every morning. He's not likely to have an accident pulling out of the driveway."

Ellen didn't have the courage to confess that she watched so she could see whether Reed drove the pickup or the Porsche. It would sound so asinine to admit she gauged their relationship by which vehicle he chose to drive that day.

"She watches because she can't bear to see him go," Derek answered when she didn't. "From everything I hear, Michelle does the same thing. What can I say? The woman's crazy about me."

"Oh, yeah?" Monte snickered. "And that's the reason she was with Rick Bloomingfield the other day."

"She was?" Derek sounded completely shocked. "There's a logical explanation for that. Michelle and I have an understanding."

"Sure you do," Monte teased. "She can date whoever she wants and you can date whoever you want. Some 'understanding.'"

To prove to the boys that she wasn't as badly smitten as they assumed—and maybe to prove the same thing to herself—Ellen didn't watch Reed leave for work the next two mornings. It was silly, anyway. So what if he drove his Porsche? He had the car, and she could see no reason for him to not drive it. Except for her unspoken insecurities. And there seemed to be plenty of those. As Derek had claimed earlier in the week, Reed could have any woman he wanted. And why he would want her was still a mystery to Ellen.

She was the first one home that afternoon. Derek was probably sorting things out with Michelle, Pat had basketball practice and no doubt Monte was in someone's kitchen.

Gathering the ingredients for her special spaghetti sauce, she arranged them neatly on the counter. She was busy reading over her recipe when the phone rang.

"Hello," she greeted cheerfully.

"This is Capitol Hill Cleaners. Mr. Morgan's tuxedo is ready."

"Pardon?" Reed hadn't told her he was having anything cleaned. Ellen usually offered to pick up his dry cleaning because it was no inconvenience to stop there on her way home from school. And she hadn't minded at all. As silly as it seemed, she'd felt very wifely doing that for him.

"Is it for Reed or Derek?" It was just like Derek to forget to mention something like that.

"The slip says it's for a Mr. Reed Morgan."

"Oh?"

"Is there a problem with picking it up early? He brought it in yesterday and told us he had to have it this evening."

This evening? Reed was going out tonight?

"From what he said, this is something special."

Well, he wouldn't wear a tuxedo to a barbecue. "I'll let him know."

"Thank you. Oh, and be sure to mention that we close at six tonight."

"Yes, I will."

A strange numbness overpowered Ellen's mind as she replaced the receiver. Something was wrong. Something was very, very wrong. Without even realizing it, she moved rapidly through the kitchen and then outside.

Repeatedly, Reed had told her the importance of reading a problem in algebra. Read it carefully, he always said, and don't make any quick assumptions. It seemed crazy to remember that now. But he was right. She couldn't jump to conclusions just because he was going out for the evening. He certainly had every right to do so. She was suddenly furious with herself. All those times he'd offered information about Danielle and she'd refused to listen, trying to play it so cool, trying to appear so blithely unconcerned when on the inside she was dying to know what he had to say.

By the time she reached the garage she was trembling, but it wasn't from the cold December air. She knew without looking that Reed had driven his sports car to work. The door creaked as she pushed it open to discover the pickup, sitting there in all its glory.

"Okay, he drove his Porsche. That doesn't have to mean anything. He isn't necessarily seeing Danielle. There's probably a logical explanation for this." Even if he was seeing Danielle, she had no right to say anything. They'd made no promises to each other.

Rubbing the chill from her bare arms, Ellen returned to the house. But the kitchen's warmth did little to chase away the bitter cold that cut her to the heart. Ellen moved numbly toward the telephone and ran her finger down the long list of numbers that hung on the wall beside it. When she located the one for Reed's office, she quickly punched out the seven numbers, then waited, her mind in turmoil.

"Mr. Morgan's office," came the efficient voice.

"Hello...this is Ellen Cunningham. I live, that is, I'm a friend of Mr. Morgan's."

"Yes, I remember seeing you the night of the Christmas party," the voice responded warmly. "We didn't have a chance to meet. Would you like me to put you through to Mr. Morgan?"

"No," she said hastily. "Could you give him a message?" Not waiting for a reply, she continued, "Tell him his tuxedo is ready at the cleaners for that... party tonight."

"Oh good, he wanted me to call. Thanks for saving me the trouble. Was there anything else?"

Moisture welled in the corners of Ellen's eyes, wetting her lashes. "No, that's it."

Being reminded by Reed's secretary that they hadn't met the night of the Christmas party forcefully brought to Ellen's attention how few of his friends she did know. None, really. He'd even gone out of his way *not* to introduce her to people.

"Just a minute," Ellen cried, her hand clenching the receiver. "There *is* something else you can tell Mr. Morgan. Tell him goodbye." With that, she severed the connection.

A tear rolled down her cheek, searing a path as it made its way to her chin. Her mind was buzzing. She'd been a fool not to have seen the situation more clearly. Reed had a good thing going, with her living at the house. She was a hair's breadth from falling in love with him. Hell, she was already there and anyone looking at her knew it. It certainly wasn't any secret from the boys. She cooked his meals, ran his errands, mended his clothes. How convenient she'd become. How handy and useful she'd been to the smooth running of his household.

But Reed had never said a word about his feelings. Sure, they'd gone out, but always to places where no one was likely to recognize him. And the one time Reed did see someone he knew, he'd pretended he wasn't with her. And when he *had* included her in a social event, he'd only introduced her to a handful of people, as though . . . as though he didn't really want others to know her. As it turned out, that evening had been a disaster, and apparently, he'd decided to take Danielle with him this time. The other woman was far more attuned to the social graces.

She'd let Reed escort Danielle tonight. Fine. But she was going to quit making life so pleasant for him. How appropriate that she now used the old servants' quarters, she thought bitterly. Because that was all she meant to him—a servant. Well, no more. She would never be content to live a backstairs life. If Reed didn't want to be seen with her, or include her in his life, that was his decision. But she couldn't . . . she *wouldn't* continue to live this way.

Without analyzing her actions, Ellen punched out a second set of numbers.

"Charlie, it's Ellen," she said quickly, doing her best to swallow back tears.

"Ellen? It doesn't sound like you."

"I know." The tightness in her chest extended all the way to her throat, choking off her breath until it escaped in a sob.

"Ellen, are you all right?"

"Yes . . . no." The fact that she'd called Charlie was a sign of her desperation. He was so sweet and she didn't want to do anything to hurt him. "Charlie, I hate to ask, but I need a friend."

"I'm here."

He said it without the least hesitation, and his unquestioning loyalty caused her to weep all the louder. "Oh, Charlie, I've got to find a place to live and I need to do it today."

"My sister's got a friend looking for a roommate. Do you want me to call her?"

"Please." Straightening, she wiped the tears from her face. Charlie might have had his faults, but he'd recognized the panic in her voice and immediately assumed control. Just now, that was what she needed—a friend to temporarily take charge of things.

"How soon can you talk to her?"

"Now. I'll call her and get right back to you. On second thought, I'll come directly to your place. If you can't stay with Patty's friend, my parents will put you up."

"Oh, Charlie, how can I ever thank you?"

The sound of his chuckle was like a clean, fresh breeze. "I'll come up with a way later." His voice softened. "You know the way I feel about you, Ellen. If you only want me for a friend, I understand. But I'm determined to be one hell of a good friend."

The back door closed with a bang. "Is anyone home?"

Guiltily, Ellen turned around, coming face to face with Monte. She replaced the telephone receiver, took a deep breath and squared her shoulders. She'd hoped to get away without having to talk to anyone.

"Ellen?" Concern clouded his youthful face. "What's wrong? You look like you've been crying." He narrowed his eyes. "You have been crying. What happened?"

"Nothing." She took a minute to wipe her nose with a tissue. "Listen, I'll be up in my room, but I'd appreciate some time alone, so don't come get me unless it's important."

"Sure. Anything you say. Are you sick? Should I call Reed?"

"No," she fairly shouted at him, then instantly regretted reacting so harshly. "Please don't contact him . . . he's busy tonight anyway." She rubbed a hand over her eyes. "And listen, about dinner—"

"Hey, don't worry. I can cook."

"You?" This wasn't the time to get into an argument. How messy he made the kitchen was no longer her concern. "There's a recipe on the counter if you want to tackle spaghetti sauce."

"Sure. I can do that. How long am I suppose to boil the noodles?"

One of her lesser concerns at the moment was boiling noodles. "Just read the back of the package."

Already he was rolling up his sleeves. "I'll take care of everything. You go lie down and do whatever it is women do when they're crying and pretending they're not."

"Right," she returned evenly. "I'll do that." Only in this case, she wasn't going to lie across her bed, burying her face in her pillow. She was going to pack up everything she owned and cart it away before Reed even had a hint she was leaving.

Sniffling as she worked, Ellen dumped the contents of her drawers into open suitcases. A couple of times she stopped to blow her nose. She detested tears. At the age of fifteen, she'd broken her leg and gritted her teeth against the agony. But she hadn't shed a tear. Now she wept as though it were the end of the world. Why, oh why, did her emotions have to be so unpredictable?

Carrying her suitcases down the first flight of stairs, she paused on the boys' floor to shift the weight of the heavy load. Because she was concentrating on her task and not watching where she was going, she walked headlong into Derek. "Sorry," she muttered.

"Ellen." He glanced at her suitcases and said her name as though he'd unexpectedly stumbled into the Queen of Sheba. "What . . . what are you doing?"

"Moving."

"Moving? But why?"

"It's a long story."

"You're crying." He sounded even more shocked by her tears than by the fact that she was moving out of the house.

"It's Reed, isn't it? What did he do?"

"He didn't do a thing. Stay out of it, Derek. I mean that."

He looked stunned. "Sure." He stepped aside and stuck his hand in his side pocket. "Anything you say."

She made a second trip downstairs, this time carting a couple of tote bags and the clothes from her closet, which she draped over the top of the two suitcases. There wasn't room in her luggage for everything. She realized she'd have to put the rest of her belongings in boxes.

Convinced she'd find a few empty cardboard boxes in the garage, she stormed through the kitchen and out the back door. Muttering between themselves, Monte and Derek followed her. Soon her movements resembled a small parade.

"Will you two stop it," she flared, whirling around and confronting them. The tears had dried now and her face burned red with the heat of anger and regret.

"We just want to know what happened," Monte interjected.

"Or is this going to be another one of your 'stay tuned' responses?" Derek asked.

"I'm moving out. I don't think I can make it any plainer than that."

"But why?"

"That's none of your business." She left them standing with mouths gaping open as she trooped up the back stairs to her rooms.

Heedlessly she tossed her things into the two boxes, more intent on escaping than on taking the proper care to ensure that nothing broke in the process. When she got to the vase that had held the roses Reed had sent her, Ellen paused and hugged it to her breast. Tears burned for release and with a monumental effort she managed to forestall them by taking in deep breaths and blinking rapidly. Setting the vase down, she decided to leave it behind. As much as possible, she wanted to leave Reed in this house and not carry the memories of him around with her like a constant, throbbing ache. That would be hard enough without taking the vase along as a constant reminder of what she'd once felt.

The scene that met her at the foot of the stairs was enough to make her stop in her tracks. The three boys were involved in a shouting match, each in turn blaming the others for Ellen's unexpected decision to move out.

"It's your fault," Derek accused Monte. "If you weren't so concerned with your stomach, she'd stay."

"My stomach? You're the one who's always asking favors of her. Like baby-sitting and cooking meals for you and your girlfriend and—"

"If you want my opinion . . ." Pat inserted.

"We don't," Monte and Derek shouted.

"Stop it. All of you," Ellen cried. "Now, if you are the least bit interested in helping me, you can take my things outside. Charlie will be here anytime."

"Charlie?" the three echoed in shock.

"Are you moving in with him?"

The suggestion was so ridiculous that she didn't bother to respond. Lugging the suitcases, the bags, two boxes and all her clothes on hangers onto the front porch, Ellen sat on the top step and waited.

She could hear the boys were pacing back and forth behind her, still bickering quietly. When the black sports car squealed around the corner, Ellen covered her face with both hands and groaned. The last person she wanted to confront now was Reed. Her throat was already swollen with the effort of not giving way to tears.

He parked in front of the house and threw open the car door.

She straightened, determined to appear cool and calm.

Abruptly Reed stopped in front of her suitcases. "What the hell is going on here?"

"Hello, Reed," she said with a breathlessness she couldn't control. "How was your day?"

He jerked his fingers through his hair as he stared back at her in utter confusion. "How the hell am I supposed to know? I get a frantic phone call from Derek telling me to get home quick. On the way out the door, my secretary hands me a message. Some absurd thing about you saying goodbye. What the bloody hell is going on? I thought you'd half killed yourself."

"I'm sorry to disappoint you."

He stalked the area in front of her twice. "Ellen, I don't know what's happening in that overworked little mind of yours, but I want some answers and I want them now."

"I'm leaving." Her hands were clenched so tight that her fingers ached.

"I'm not blind," he shouted, quickly losing control of his obviously limited patience. "I can see that. I'm asking you why."

Pride demanded that she raise her chin and meet his probing gaze. "I've decided I'm an unstable person," she told him, her voice low and quavering. "I broke my leg once and didn't shed a tear, but when I learn that you're going to a party tonight, I start to cry."

"Ellen." He said her name gently, then shook his head as if clearing his thoughts. "You're not making any sense."

"I know it. That's the worst part."

"In the simplest terms possible, tell me why you're leaving."

"I'm trying." Furious with herself, she wiped a tear from her cheek. How could she explain it to him when everything was still so muddled in her own mind? "I'm leaving because you're driving the Porsche."

"What!" he exploded.

"I told you I'm an unstable person."

He rubbed a hand along the back of his neck and exhaled sharply. "I'm beginning to believe you."

"All right," she burst out. "You tell me. Why did you drive the Porsche today?"

"Would you believe that my truck was low on gas?"

"I may be unstable," she cried, "but I'm not stupid. You're going out with Danielle. Not that I care, mind you."

"I can tell." His mocking gaze lingered on her suitcases. "I hate to disappoint you, but Danielle won't be with me."

She didn't know whether to believe him or not. "It doesn't matter."

"None of this is making sense."

"I don't imagine it would. Really, I apologize for acting like such an unreasonable woman, but that's exactly the way I feel. So, I'm getting out of here with my pride intact."

"Is your pride worth so much?"

"It's the only thing I have left," she said simply. She'd already given him her heart.

"She's moving in with Charlie," Derek inserted in a concerned voice. "You aren't going to let her go, are you, Reed?"

"You can't," Monte added.

"He won't," Pat stated confidently.

For a moment, the three of them stared intently at Reed. Ellen noticed the way his green eyes hardened to points of steel. "Yes I can," he said at last. "If this is the way you want it, then so be it. Goodbye, Ellen." With that, he marched back into the house.

CHAPTER TEN

"I'M SWEARING OFF MEN for good," Ellen vowed, taking another long swallow of the pink Chablis.

"Me, too," Darlene, her new roommate, echoed. To toast the promise, Darlene bent forward to touch the rim of her wineglass against Ellen's and missed. A shocked moment passed before the two broke into hysterical laughter.

"Here." Ellen replenished their half-full glasses as tears of mirth rolled down her face. The world seemed to spin off its axis for a moment as she straightened. "You know what? I think we're drunk."

"Maybe you are," Darlene declared, slurring her words, "but not me. I can hold my wine as well as any man can."

"I thought we weren't going to talk about men anymore."

"Right, I forgot."

"Do you think they're talking about us?" Ellen asked, putting a hand to her head in an effort to keep the walls from going around and around.

"Naw, we're just a fading memory to those bums."

"Right." Ellen pointed her index finger toward the ceiling in emphatic agreement.

The doorbell chimed and both women stared accusingly at the door, as though it were the source of all their problems. "If it's a man, don't answer it."

"Right again." Ellen staggered across the beige carpet. The floor seemed to pitch under her feet and she put a hand on the back of the sofa to steady herself. Facing the door, she turned around abruptly. "How do I know if it's a man or not?"

The doorbell sounded again, in short irritated beeps.

Darlene motioned languidly with her hand to show that she no longer cared who was at the door. "Just open it."

Holding the knob in a death grip, Ellen pulled open the door and found herself glaring at solid male chest. "It's a man," she announced to Darlene.

"Who?"

Squinting her eyes, Ellen studied the blurred male figure who dominated the doorway, and she recognized Monte. "Monte," she cried, instantly sobering. "What are you doing here?"

"I . . . I was in the neighborhood and thought I'd stop in and see how you're doing."

"Come in." She stepped aside to let him enter. "What brings you to this neck of the woods?" She hiccuped despite her frenzied effort to look sober. "It's a school night. You shouldn't be out this late."

"It's only ten-thirty. You've been drinking." He made it sound as though she were sitting in the middle of an opium den.

"Me?" She slammed her hand against her chest. "Have we been drinking, Darlene?"

Her roommate grabbed the wine bottle from the tabletop and hid it behind her back. "Not us."

Monte cast them a look of utter disbelief. "How'd your exams go?" he asked Ellen politely.

"Fine," she answered and hiccuped again. Embarrassed, she covered her mouth with her hand. "I think."

"What about algebra?"

"I'm making it by the skin of my nose."

"Teeth," both Darlene and Monte corrected.

"Right."

Looking uncomfortable, Monte added, "Maybe I should come back another time."

"Okay." Ellen wasn't about to look a gift horse in the mouth. If she was going to run into her former housemates, then she'd prefer to do it when she looked and felt her best. Definitely not when she was feeling...tipsy and the walls kept spinning. But on second thought, she couldn't resist inquiring about the others. "How's... everyone?"

"Fine." But he lowered his gaze to the carpet. "Not really, if you want the truth."

A shaft of fear went through her, tempering the effects of several glasses of wine. "It's not Reed, is it? Is he ill?"

"No, Reed's fine, I guess. He hasn't been around much lately."

No doubt he was spending a lot of his time at parties and social events with Danielle. Or with any number of other women, all of them far more sophisticated than Ellen.

"Things haven't been the same since you left," Monte added sheepishly.

"Who's doing the cooking?"

He shrugged his shoulders dramatically. "We've more or less been taking turns."

"That sounds fair." She hoped that in the months she'd lived with them the three boys had at least learned their way around the kitchen.

"Derek started a fire yesterday."

Ellen struggled to conceal her dismay. "Was there any damage?" As much as she tried to persuade herself that she didn't need to feel guilty over leaving the boys, this news was her undoing. "Was anyone hurt?" she gasped out.

"Not really, and Reed assured us the insurance would take care of everything."

"What happened?" Ellen was almost afraid to ask.

"Nothing much. Derek forgot to turn off the burner and the grease caught on fire. Then he tried to beat it out with a dish towel, but that burst into flames, too. But the real mistake was throwing the burning towel into the sink because when he tossed it, the towel lit the curtains."

"Oh, good grief." Ellen sank her head into her hands.

"It's not too bad, really. Reed said he wanted new kitchen walls anyway."

"The walls too?"

"Well, the curtains started the wallpaper on fire."

Ellen wished she hadn't asked. "Was anyone burned?"

Monte moved a bandaged hand from behind his back. "Just me, but only a little."

"Oh, Monte," she cried, fighting back an attack of guilt. "What did you do—try and pound out the fire with your fist?" Leave it to Monte. He'd probably tried to rescue whatever it was Derek had been cooking.

"No, I grabbed a hot biscuit from the oven and blistered one finger."

"Then why did you wrap up your whole hand?" From the size of the bandage, it looked as though he'd been lucky not to lose his arm.

"I thought you might feel sorry for me and come back."

"Oh, Monte." Gently, she reached up to brush the hair from his temple.

"I didn't realize what a good cook you were until you left. I kept thinking that maybe it was something I'd done that caused you to leave."

"Of course not."

"Then you'll come back and cook dinners again?"

Good ol' Monte never forgot about his stomach. "The four of you will do fine without me."

"You mean you won't come back?"

"I can't." She felt like crying all the more. But she struggled to hold back the tears that were stinging her eyes. "I'm really sorry, but I can't."

Hanging his head so low that his chin touched his collarbone, Monte nodded. "Well, have a merry Christmas anyway."

"Right. You, too."

"Bye, Ellen." He turned back to the door, his large hand gripping the knob. "You know about Pat making varsity, don't you?"

She'd read it in the *Daily*. "I'm really proud of him. You tell him for me. Okay?"

"Sure."

She closed the door after him and leaned against it while the regrets washed over her like a torrent of rain. Holding back the tears was difficult, but somehow she managed. She'd shed enough tears. It was time to put her grief behind her and to start facing life again.

"I take it Monte is one of the guys," Darlene remarked. She set the wine back on the table, but neither seemed interested in indulging in another glass.

Ellen nodded. "The one with the stomach."

"But he's so skinny."

"I know. There's no justice in this world." But she wasn't talking about Monte's appetite in relation to his weight. She was talking about Reed. If she'd held any hopes that he really did care for her, those had vanished in the past week. He hadn't even tried to get in touch with her. She knew he wouldn't have had any problem locating her. The obvious conclusion was that he didn't *want* to see her again. At first she thought he might have believed the boys' ridiculous claim that she was moving in with Charlie. But if he'd loved her half as much as she loved him, even that shouldn't have stopped him from coming after her.

Apparently, presuming that Reed cared for her was a basic mistake on her part. She hadn't heard a sound from him all week. Exam week, at that. Well fine, she'd decided. She'd wipe him out of her memory—just as effectively as she forgot every algebraic formula she ever learned. A giggle escaped and Darlene tossed her a curious look. Ellen carried their wineglasses to the sink, ignoring her new roommate, as she mused on her dilemma. The trouble was, she wanted to remember the algebra, which seemed to slip out of her mind as soon as it entered, and she wanted to forget Reed, who never left her thoughts for an instant.

"I think I'll go to bed," Darlene said, holding her hand to her stomach. "I'm not feeling so great."

"Me neither." But Ellen's churning stomach had little to do with the wine. "'Night."

"I'll see you in the morning."

Ellen nodded. She was fortunate to have found Darlene. The other woman, who had recently broken up with her fiancé after a two-year engagement, understood how Ellen felt. It seemed natural that they drown their sorrows together. But damn it all, she missed the boys and...Reed.

One thing she'd learned from this experience was that men and school didn't mix. Darlene might not have been serious about swearing off men, but Ellen was. She was through with them for good—or at least until she obtained her degree. For now, she was determined to bury herself in her books, get her teaching credentials and then become the best first-grade teacher around.

Only, she couldn't close her eyes without remembering Reed's touch or how he'd slip up behind her and wrap her in his arms. Something as simple as a passing glance from him had been enough to thrill her. Well, that relationship was over—ruined. And just in the nick of time. She could have been hurt. Really hurt. She could be feeling terrible. Really terrible. Just like she did now.

SIGNS OF CHRISTMAS were everywhere Ellen looked. Huge weatherproof decorations adorned the streetlights down University Way. Store windows were painted in a variety of Christmas themes, and the streets were jammed with holiday traffic. Ellen tried to absorb some of the good cheer that surrounded her, with little success.

The following morning she planned to leave for Yakima. But instead of feeling the pull toward home and family, Ellen's thoughts drifted to Reed and the boys. They had been her surrogate family since September and she couldn't erase them from her mind as easily as she'd hoped.

As she walked across campus, sharp gusts of wind mussed her hair and caused her to cast her eyes downward. Her face felt numb with cold. All day she'd been debating about what to do with the Christmas gifts she'd bought for the boys. Her first inclination had been to deliver them herself—when Reed wasn't home, of course. But just the thought of returning to the lovely old house had proved so painful that Ellen abandoned the thought.

Instead, Darlene had promised to deliver them the next day, after Ellen had left for Yakima.

Hugging the books against her chest, Ellen trudged toward the bus stop. According to her watch, she had about ten minutes to wait. Now her feet felt as numb as her face. She frowned at her open-toed pumps, cursing the decrees of fashion and her insane willingness to wear "cute" shoes at this time of year. It wasn't as though a handsome prince were likely to come galloping by only to be overwhelmed by her attractive toes. Even if one did swoop Ellen and her frozen toes onto his silver steed, she'd be highly suspicious of his character.

Swallowing a giggle, she took a shortcut across the lawn in the Quad.

"Is something funny?"

A pair of men's leather loafers had joined her fashionable gray pumps, matching her stride step for step. Stunned, Ellen glanced upward. Reed.

"Well?" he asked again in an achingly gentle voice. "Something seems to amuse you."

"My...shoes. I was thinking about attracting a prince...a man." Oh heavens, why had she said that? "That is," she mumbled on, trying to cover her embarrassment, "my feet are numb."

"You need to get out of the cold." His hands were thrust into his pockets and he was so compellingly handsome that Ellen forced her eyes away. If she stared at him long enough, she feared, she'd give him whatever he asked. The way his face had looked the last time she'd seen him was seared into her memory for all time. She remembered how steely and cold his eyes had became the day she'd announced she was moving out. One word from him and she would have stayed. If only he'd explained. Hell, the "might-have-beens" didn't matter anymore. He hadn't asked her to stay and so she'd gone. Pure and simple. Or so it had seemed at the time.

Determination thickened her trembling voice as she finally spoke. "The bus will be at the corner in seven minutes."

Her statement was met with silence. Together they reached the sidewalk and strolled toward the sheltered bus area.

Much as she wished to appear cool and composed, Ellen's gaze was riveted on the tall, somber man at her side. She noticed how straight and dark Reed's brows were and how his chin jutted out with stubborn male pride. Every line of his beloved face emanated strength and unflinching resolve.

Abruptly, she looked away. Pride was no stranger to her, either. Her methods might have been wrong, she told herself, but she'd been right to let Reed know he'd hurt her. She wasn't willing to continue being a victim of her love for him.

"Ellen," he said softly, "I was hoping we could talk."

She made a show of glancing at her wristwatch. "Go ahead. You've got six and a half minutes."

"Here?"

"As you so recently stated, I need to get out of the cold."

"I'll take you to lunch."

"I'm not hungry." To further her embarrassment, her stomach growled and she pressed a firm hand over it, commanding it to be quiet.

"When was the last time you ate a decent meal?"

"Yesterday. No," she corrected, "today."

"Come on, we're getting out of here."

"No way."

"I'm not arguing with you, Ellen. I've given you a week to come to your senses. I still haven't figured out what went wrong. And I'm not waiting any longer for the answers. Got that?"

Stubbornly she ignored him, looking instead in the direction of the traffic. She could see the bus approaching, though it was still several blocks away. "I believe everything that needed to be said—" she motioned dramatically with her hand "—was already said."

"And what's this I hear about you succumbing to the demon rum?"

"I was only a little drunk," she spat out, furious at Monte's loose tongue. "Darlene and I were celebrating. We've sworn off men for life." Or at least until Reed freely admitted that he loved her and needed her. At the moment it didn't appear likely.

"I see." His eyes seemed to be looking all the way into her soul. "If that's the way you want it, fine. Just answer a couple of questions and I'll leave you alone. Agreed?"

"All right."

"First, what the hell were you talking about when you flew off the handle about me driving the Porsche?"

"Oh, that." Now it just seemed silly.

"Yes, that."

"Well, you only drove the Porsche when you were seeing Danielle."

"But I wasn't. It's been over between us ever since the night of the Christmas party."

"It has?" She realized that the words came out in a squeak.

Reed dragged his fingers through his hair. "I haven't seen Danielle in weeks."

Resolutely Ellen dropped her gaze to the sidewalk. "But the cleaners phoned with that business about the tuxedo. You were attending some fancy party."

"So? I wasn't taking another woman."

"It doesn't matter," she insisted stubbornly. "You weren't taking me, either."

"Of course not," he shouted, his raised voice attracting the attention of several passersby. "You were studying for exams. I couldn't very well ask you to attend an extremely boring business dinner with me. Not when you were spending every available minute hitting the books." He lowered his voice to a calm, even pitch.

The least he could do was be more unreasonable, Ellen thought irritably. She simply wasn't in the mood for logic.

"Did you hear what I said?"

The sheer force of his will demanded that she nod. She did.

"There is only one woman in my life. You. To be honest, Ellen, I can't understand any of this. You may be many things, but you're not the jealous type. I've wanted to talk about Danielle with you. Any other woman would have loved hearing all the details. But not you." His voice was only slightly raised. "Then when you throw up these ridiculous accusations about the truck and the Porsche, I'm at a loss to understand you."

Oh Lord, now she felt even more of a fool. "Then why were you driving the Porsche?" Her arms tightened around her books. "Forget I asked that."

"You really have a thing for that sports car, don't you?"

"It's not the car."

"I'm glad to hear that."

Squaring her shoulders, Ellen decided it was time to be forthright and honest, time to face things squarely rather than skirt around them. "My feelings are that you would rather not be seen with me," she said bluntly.

"What?" he exploded.

"You kept taking me to these out-of-the-way restaurants."

"I did it to be alone with you."

"Ha! You didn't want to be seen with me," she countered.

"I can't believe this." He took three steps away from her, then turned around sharply.

"Don't you think the Des Moines Marina is a bit far to go for a meal?"

"I was afraid we'd run into one of the boys."

More logic, and she was in no mood for it. "Try to deny not introducing me to your friend the night we went to that French film."

His eyes narrowed. "You can damn well bet I wasn't going to introduce you to Tom Dailey. He's a lecher. I was protecting you."

"What about the night of the Christmas party? You only introduced me to a handful of people."

"Of course. Every man in the place was looking for an excuse to take you away from me. I was keeping you to myself. If you'd wanted to flirt with the others, you should have said something."

"I only wanted to be with you."

"Then why bring up that evening now?"

"I was offended."

"I apologize," he shouted.

"Fine."

The bus arrived, its doors parting with a swish. But Ellen didn't move. Reed's gaze commanded her to stay with him, and she was torn. Her strongest impulse, though, was not to board the bus. It didn't matter that she was cold and the wind was cutting through her thin coat or that she could barely feel her big toe. Her heart was telling her one thing and her head another.

"You coming or not, miss?" the driver called out to her.

"She won't be taking the bus," Reed answered, slipping his hand under her elbow. "She's coming with me."

"Whatever." The door swished shut and the bus roared away, leaving a trail of black diesel smoke in its wake.

"You are coming with me, aren't you?" he coaxed.

"I suppose."

His hand was at the small of her back, directing her across the busy street to a coffee shop, festooned with tinsel and tired-looking decorations. "I wasn't kidding about lunch."

"When was the last time *you* had a decent meal?" she couldn't resist asking.

"About a week ago," he grumbled. "Derek's cooking is a poor substitute for real food."

They found a table in the back of the café. The waitress handed them each a menu and filled their water glasses.

"I heard about the fire."

Reed groaned. "That was a comedy of errors."

"Is there much damage?"

"Enough." The look he gave her was mildly accusing.

The guilt returned. Trying to disguise it, Ellen made a show of glancing through the menu. The last thing on her mind at the moment was food. When the waitress returned, Ellen ordered the special of the day without knowing what it was. The day was destined to be full of surprises.

"Ellen," Reed began, then cleared his throat. "Come back."

Her heart melted at the hint of anguish in his low voice. Her gaze was magnetically drawn to his. She wanted to tell him how much she longed to be...home. She wanted to say that the house on Capitol Hill was the only real home she had now, that she longed to walk through its front door again. With him.

"Nothing has been the same since you left."

The knot in her stomach pushed its way up to her throat, choking off her breath.

"The boys are miserable."

Resolutely she shook her head. If she went back, it had to be for Reed and not on account of the boys.

"Why not?"

Tears blurred her vision. "Because."

"That makes about as much sense as you being angry because I drove the Porsche." His clipped reply conveyed the depth of his irritation.

Taking several deep, measured breaths, Ellen shook her head. "If all you need is a cook, I can suggest several who—"

"I don't give a damn about the cooking."

The café went silent as every head turned curiously in their direction. "I wasn't taking about the cooking *here*," Reed explained to the room full of shocked faces.

The normal noise of the café resumed.

"Good grief, Ellen, you've got me so tied up in knots I'm about to get kicked out of here."

"Me, tie you in knots?" She was amazed Reed felt she had that much power over him.

"If you won't come back for the boys, will you consider doing it for me?" The intense green eyes demanded a response.

"I want to know why you want me back. So I can cook your meals and—"

"I don't give a damn if you never do another thing around the house. I want you there because I love you. Damn it."

Her dark eyes widened. "You love me, damn it?"

"You're not making this any easier." He ripped the napkin from around the silverware and slammed it down on his lap. "You must have known. I didn't bother keeping it secret."

"You didn't bother keeping it secret . . . from anyone but me," she repeated hotly.

"Come on. Don't tell me you didn't know."

"I didn't know."

"Well, you do now," he yelled back.

The waitress cautiously approached their table, standing back until Reed glanced irritably in her direction. Hurriedly the teenaged girl set their plates in front of them and promptly moved away.

"You frightened her," Ellen accused.

"I'm the one in a panic here. Do you or do you not love me?"

Again, it seemed as though the entire customer population paused, awaiting her reply.

"You'd best answer him, miss," the elderly gentleman sitting at the table next to theirs suggested. "Fact is, we're all curious."

"Yes, I love him."

Reed cast her a look of utter disbelief. "You'll tell a stranger but not me?"

"I love you, Reed Morgan. There, are you happy?"

"Overjoyed."

"I can tell." Ellen had thought that when she admitted her feelings, Reed would jump up from the table and throw his arms around her. Instead, he looked as angry as she'd ever seen him.

"I think you'd better ask her to marry you while she's in a friendly mood," the older man suggested next.

"Well?" Reed looked at her. "What do you think?"

"You want to get married?"

"It's the time of year to be generous," the waitress offered. "He's handsome enough."

"He is, isn't he?" Ellen agreed, her sense of humor restored by this unexpected turn of events. "But he's a little hard to understand at times."

"All men are, believe me," a woman customer from across the room shouted. "But he looks like a decent sort. Go ahead and give him another chance."

The anger washed from Reed's dark eyes as he reached for Ellen's hand. "I love you. I want to marry you. Won't you put me out of my misery?"

Tears dampened her eyes as she nodded wildly.

"Let's go home." Standing, Reed took out his wallet and threw some money on the table.

Ellen quickly buttoned her jacket and picked up her purse. "Goodbye, everyone," she called with a cheerful wave. "Thank you—and Merry Christmas!"

The amused customers broke into a round of applause as Reed took Ellen's hand and pulled her outside.

She was no sooner out the door when Reed hauled her into his arms. "Oh Lord, Ellen, I've missed you and your cotton-candy kisses."

Reveling in the warmth of his arms, she nuzzled closer. "I've missed you, too. I've even missed the boys."

"As far as I'm concerned, they're on their own. I want you back for myself. That house was full of people, yet it's never felt so empty." Suddenly he looked around, as though he'd only now realized that their private moment was taking place in the middle of a busy street. "Let's get out of here." He slipped an arm about her waist, steering her toward the campus parking lot. "But I think I'd better tell you something important."

"What?" Her eyes glowed with an inner sparkle as she glanced up at him.

"I didn't bring the truck."

"Oh?" She swallowed down the disappointment. She could try, but she doubted that she would ever be the Porsche type.

"I traded in the truck last week."

"For what?" Her eyes widened with dismay.

"Maybe it was presumptuous of me, but I was hoping you'd accept my marriage proposal."

"What's the truck got to do with whether I marry you or not?"

"*You're* asking me that? The very woman who left me—"

"All right, all right, I get the picture."

"I traded it in for a station wagon. A family wagon that's waiting to be filled with children."

"Oh, Reed." With a small cry of joy, she flung her arms around this man she knew she would love for a lifetime. No matter what car he drove.

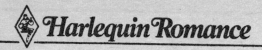 **Harlequin Romance**

Coming Next Month

Available in June wherever paperback books are sold, or
through Harlequin Reader Service.

In the U.S.
901 Fuhrmann Blvd.
P.O. Box 1397
Buffalo, N.Y. 14240-1397

In Canada
P.O. Box 603
Fort Erie, Ontario
L2A 5X3

ATTRACTIVE, SPACE SAVING BOOK RACK

Display your most prized novels on this handsome and sturdy book rack. The hand-rubbed walnut finish will blend into your library decor with quiet elegance, providing a practical organizer for your favorite hard-or soft-covered books.

Only $9.95

Approximately 16" x 8" when assembled

Assembles in seconds!

To order, rush your name, address and zip code, along with a check or money order for $10.70* ($9.95 plus 75¢ postage and handling) payable to *Harlequin Reader Service*:

Harlequin Reader Service
Book Rack Offer
901 Fuhrmann Blvd.
P.O. Box 1396
Buffalo, NY 14269-1396

Offer not available in Canada.

BKR-1A

*New York and Iowa residents add appropriate sales tax.